Living in Your Light

Living in Your Light

A NOVEL

ABDELLAH TAÏA

translated by

EMMA RAMADAN

SEVEN STORIES PRESS
NEW YORK • OAKLAND

This work received support for excellence in publication and translation from Albertine Translation, a program created by Villa Albertine and funded by Albertine Foundation.

Seven Stories Press
140 Watts Street
New York, NY 10013
www.sevenstories.com

Library of Congress Cataloging-in-Publication Data

Names: Taïa, Abdellah, 1973- author. | Ramadan, Emma, translator.
Title: Living in your light / Abdellah Taïa ; translated by Emma Ramadan.
Other titles: Vivre à ta lumière. English
Description: New York : Seven Stories Press, 2025.
Identifiers: LCCN 2024043473 | ISBN 9781644214534 (trade paperback) | ISBN 9781644214541 (ebook)
Subjects: LCGFT: Novels.
Classification: LCC PQ3989.2.T27 V5813 2025 | DDC 843/.92--dc23/eng/20241214
LC record available at https://lccn.loc.gov/2024043473

College professors and high school and middle school teachers may order free examination copies of Seven Stories Press titles. Visit https://www.sevenstories.com/pg/resources-academics or email academic@sevenstories.com.

Printed in the United States of America

9 8 7 6 5 4 3 2 1

For my mother, M'Barka Allali (1930–2010).

This book comes entirely from you.

Its heroine, Malika, speaks and shouts with your voice.

1

Béni Mellal

*

ALL THE LOVE OF THIS EARTH.

All the love that there is on this earth will not be enough for me, will not help me to bear what happens to me after you, Allal.

You went so far away, to a world I know nothing about. And you will not return.

There is nothing ahead of me now but memory, absence, love without you.

You watched me for months and months when I went to the souk with my father. You weren't afraid of him and you let your eyes speak, follow me, enter me, and decide for me what would follow, happen. Be with you. Be yours. Be your wife. Your eyes didn't say that I was beautiful nor that you were in love with me. No, none of that. Your eyes played, danced, and invited me to do the same. Dance with you in public, in the souk. That was what you wanted, what excited you. To see how I would react, what I would show of myself. My reaction to your stares when my father was right there, beside me. Together we carry a basket of vegetables, he and I. We are perfectly respectable. Was my father unaware? I don't think so. He plays innocent, my father. But he's tender. Tender and submissive to his second wife. It's only in this souk, once per week, that I can have him all to myself. It's only here that he dares show me any affection and buys me donuts coated with sugar.

You had planned your strategy, Allal. You went for it, you spoke. Not to me, no. To my father who, for some time, had been trying to get rid of me. Me, Malika, his daughter. He couldn't take it anymore, watching his second wife humiliate me every day and saying nothing about it.

He said nothing, my father. He was enchanted by her, bewitched. He'd lost his head a long time ago. He let himself be guided, directed. I was his weak point. The daughter of his first marriage.

She grew up, little Malika. Seventeen years old. She's a woman now. Entirely a woman. She must be given to someone. Find her a man. There are plenty in this vast *bled* where everyone keeps tabs on everyone else.

Let me help you carry the second basket, my uncle.

That's how you approached us, Allal.

It's too heavy for you and your daughter, my uncle.

Okay, my son. May God show you the path to paradise, my son.

You were walking on the other side. My father was between us. You acted like manly men, you spoke of crops, of the sky that had been generous with rain that year, and of the French who still didn't want to leave Morocco. You spoke of the facts of life that I didn't yet know about. And suddenly, my father stopped and said:

You're the son of Saleh, aren't you?

How had he guessed? I never would have known.

I am the youngest son of Saleh, yes. I am Allal, my uncle.

Allal. That's right. Little Allal. How you've grown! You don't remember him, Malika? Look. It's Allal. Give him your hand and greet him. Allal is like a cousin to you. Give him your hand. Don't be shy. Allal is from the same place as us, from the same extended family as us. Same blood and same flesh. Look at him. I am here with you, Malika. Look at Allal. He has become a man. Bigger than me. Look.

Later, I understood that my father knew all about my little game. He had seen everything. My little dances for you, Allal. Your eyes permanently fixed on me. Your eyes devouring me.

It was my father, Baba, who insisted on bringing me with him to the souk, and he was the one who wanted to buy me donuts each time from the old woman set up next to a little open-air café. Your café, Allal.

You were there. In that café. You were always there.

I am standing near the old woman's stall. I am alone. Baba told me he would be back in about ten minutes. I eat the donuts very slowly. I take my time. I let you look at me all you want. My body. My character. My history. I am strong. That is what you will love about me. A strong woman who engulfs you entirely. Not a woman just for a night. No. I am a woman for something serious, you see that, a woman to accompany you and help you as you face off against *zman*, time, which passes and ends up ruining us all. I am Malika. I am in very good health. I am not lazy. I see things through. I have good teeth. My hair is very black. My thighs are solid. My chest will continue to grow, don't worry. My stomach is large. And my Berber tattoo between the eyes means one thing: I am loyal. Loyal and cunning, to be frank. But I imagine that doesn't scare you, my cunning. You continue to watch me, you don't judge me. I please you. I please you, I know it. Look, Allal. Look. I've finished eating the second donut. I start on the third. I want you to see that I have a healthy appetite. I eat. I eat. I love food, all kinds of food. I am a woman who is not ashamed to eat. Malika. Malika, Allal. It's for you. Come. Come. When will you come?

You walk with us, Allal. Down our path. You help us, me and Baba. You carry the second basket. And you speak. You have a lot to say. I barely listen. I let myself be soothed by the sound of your voice. I enter into that voice and its world. My father is delighted. He has understood that you are a man who is not afraid. A man full of words that ring true and good stories to share. A man who reveals himself all at once, who is open, who says: Here is my heart.

Hope exists. With your body, Allal, in your heart, Allal, I will find another path. Finally flee my stepmother and her maliciousness. Thwart destiny. Grab hold of hope, have proof of it.

I will live.

Baba suddenly asks you that question, direct, too direct:

What do you have in life, my son Allal?

You answer honestly. You don't even stop to think.

I have nothing but my open-air café, my uncle. I bring it with me from souk to souk, from mausoleum to mausoleum. It's not much, I know. It's no guarantee of a beautiful future, I know. But I live well, even very well during the summer, with this café. I've managed to save up a bit of money. I live with my parents. In their house. And I have two brothers who are younger than me. I am twenty-seven years old, my uncle. It is time for me to get married. I have cousins younger than me who already have children. I want to get married.

I daydream. I look at your feet, Allal. Your feet in leather sandals. They are dirty, your feet. Strong and dirty. I want to take them in my hands, those feet, right there, on the spot. Wash them slowly, gently, very gently. And then massage them with olive oil. I know how. I practice on my father's feet when he comes home at night from working in the field. Isn't that right, Baba? Tell Allal that I know how to massage feet. Tell him. Tell him. This detail is very important. Men's feet. Allal's feet. I will always begin with your feet, Allal. And then everything will be easy. Love. Love.

The dream of love.

We've arrived at our house. We're in front of the door. You place the basket on the ground. My father invites you in for a cup of mint tea. You say that you have to return to the souk to pack up your café. Baba insists:

At least a glass of water, Allal.

You accept.

Bring him a glass of water, my daughter Malika.

It's only you and me now. Baba has gone to bring the baskets inside the house. He'll be back any minute now.

You drink the water. You're very thirsty. I watch you drink the entire glass in one gulp. Your eyes are closed. Your head is tilted back. I see your strong neck. I see everything, everything, from close up. Heat rises in me. The dark black hairs of your short beard. Your nose, long and thin. Your lips, the color of the land here: red ocher. Your ears, huge and strange. Your head is almost shaved, like a thief's. You never let your hair grow, I believe. Why not?

I want to reach out my hand and caress your head.

You are a man. You are handsome. I find you handsome. I tell you this, in my heart: You are so handsome, Allal.

Did you hear me?

You are handsome. You are not rich but you are handsome.

I breathe in the smell of your body, Allal. The body of a man beaten by the sun for years and years, browned by the sun, almost black from the sun. A body that's sweating, dripping. It is hot. It is cold. It is burning.

Allal, you come toward me. Open your legs, you say. Open them. Open, Malika.

I open them. Immediately. For you. I have been waiting for so long. I am seventeen years old. It is time. To give myself to you, Allal. Take you inside me, mix together our scents and our sweat. Our paths.

And our dreams.

You have finished drinking the water, Allal. You make no improper or uncalled-for gesture. You're in front of Baba's house. I emerge from my dream beside your body. I lower my eyes. You hand me the glass. Your hand touches my hand. It lasts three or four seconds. Your heat, Allal. The heat on the surface of your skin. It enters me and courses through all of me, from my head to my toes. You say goodbye.

Bsslama, Malika.

Bsslama, Allal.

You leave. Right away. I watch you leave. You walk. You walk quickly. You are so light. You are skinny. You are fragile. You are a little bird. I am stronger than you.

You turned left. You disappeared from my sight. But you are still here, in the air. I see you. Your trace. Your memory. Your gentle virility.

Baba returns.

Come in, Malika. Come in, my little girl. Allal is a fine man. It's in God's hands now.

You came back to see us a month later to ask for my hand. Both of your parents were with you. And your best friend too: Merzougue. He's my brother, more than my brother, I heard you say to my father when you introduced him. Merzougue. Sometimes, a friend is much better than a brother, you're right, Allal.

Merzougue was seated next to you, glued to you. When I entered the living room of our house to serve everyone mint tea, Merzougue said:

She's lucky, your daughter.

Baba didn't ask for much money as a dowry. Almost nothing. But to your parents, Allal, he spoke from the heart:

Malika will be your daughter. I give her to you. I am not selling her. I am entrusting her to you. I am not forcing Malika to do anything. She is your daughter. Life will smile on her with you and your son Allal. Life will finally reward her. I am counting on you.

Hearing these words, my stepmother stood up and left the living room. She wanted to show her disapproval of Baba's words and what he was implying. I went to check whether or not the couscous was ready.

Baba continued his speech.

My daughter Malika lost her mother at a very young age. I couldn't raise her on my own. In this life, a man cannot weather the storm without a wife. I married again. I had no choice.

Your father then began speaking.

You daughter Malika will be our daughter. Do not worry. And our son Allal is your son. God will guide us on this path as good Muslims with pure hearts. But . . . but . . .

But what?

The dowry is a bit too substantial for our son.

How much money can you give for my daughter?

This isn't about money. Trust is the most important thing.

How much?

That's for you to decide. Our son is a good son. A man. He is not afraid of work. He is—

How much?

Half of what you asked.

Baba turned toward me. He took my hand in his.

Malika, my daughter, you have heard what has just been said. Are you okay with all of this? I am not forcing you to do anything. Do you want to marry Allal under these conditions? You won't tell me later that I sold you for nothing? Allal is here, in front of you. His parents are here, in front of you. You have heard everything they said. Their proposition. Money isn't everything in life, but . . . but sometimes you have to know . . .

I am okay with it, Baba. I want to marry Allal. I accept what his parents propose.

You have all heard it. My daughter Malika agrees. She is your daughter now. She is yours. She is yours, my son Allal. We will celebrate the wedding in a month. Now let's read Surah Al-Fatiha, since we are all in agreement.

Listening to these words, I looked at you, Allal.

You didn't look at me at that moment, Allal.

You turned toward your friend Merzougue and you gave each other a very warm embrace. Two friends. Two brothers.

And I understood, seeing you entwined like that for a long time, too long, that there was a secret between you. A very special bond.

Baba was even forced to intervene. He said to you:

That's enough now, Allal my son. Let go of Merzougue and give Malika a kiss on the head.

You kissed me timidly in front of everyone.

Merzougue smiled wide and warmly encouraged you.

You returned to Merzougue. You looked at each other. You were excited. You embraced again. You were entwined again. In front of us all. You were not ashamed.

What am I supposed to do, I thought, faced with such a spectacle? Who is marrying whom here?

I understand and I don't understand. I see and I don't see. The world of men from the bled. Solidarity between men of the bled. The gestures of men. Men spend the majority of their time together. Man to man. And what happens happens. They touch each other. While they wait. Nothing new. It's natural. Allal and Merzougue, it's natural. One shouldn't ask too many questions.

Allal has a friend and a supporter: Merzougue. I shouldn't take that away from him. I am not the only person in Allal's life and heart.

I am not jealous of Merzougue. Do you hear me, Allal? Even when I saw you together with my own eyes on the terrace of the house, on top of each other, naked, naked, I did not become jealous. It was night. Summer. It was too hot. That's all. I wasn't shocked. I wasn't devastated. I know what life is like. The facts of life.

Merzougue was here long before me.

Merzougue is not a dangerous man. When he looks at me, his eyes don't change. His eyes are always full of tenderness.

Merzougue is all that's left to me now that you're gone, Allal. When I see him, I see you. I make him food. I invite him over. He comes. He eats like you, has the same mannerisms as you. He eats for you, in memory of you. I don't cry.

Merzougue predicted what was going to happen in Indochina. He did everything to stop you from going there, so far away, so far away, to fight for the French, to fight against people you didn't even know, to kill people who had done nothing to you. You wouldn't hear any of it.

I'll bring back money, a lot of money. And life will be good for the three of us. You, Malika. You, Merzougue. And me, with you. We'll move out of my parents' house. We'll be free from my parents. We'll buy land that we'll cultivate. And we'll have lots of children. Many, many children. We'll be comfortable, you'll see. I'll wage their war and I'll take their money. That's my mission.

How naive you were, Allal. And how I regret not having followed my intuition: to do everything I could to stop you from walking into your own death. Death in a land that doesn't exist for us, a country that isn't real to us.

We listened to you, Allal. You dreamt and constructed a prosperous future for us, in front of us. You convinced us. No, that's not true. You ate our brains. We let you leave.

Where is Allal?

Allal is in Indochina.

Any news from Allal?

Allal died in Indochina.

Indochina. Weeks and weeks of traveling by boat. Months, perhaps. A boat that walks on water.

You will be afraid, Allal.

I won't be alone, Malika. Other Moroccans will be with me. There will even be men from our bled with me.

You will kill people, Allal.

I know.

Take lives, Allal.

I'm not an idiot, Malika. I'm going to war. I understand what's in store for me.

We don't need this, my Allal. We'll find another solution. We've only been married a year. We're still young. In very good health.

You want to keep living here in my parents' house? You want to keep being a maid and a slave for my parents and my brothers? Have you forgotten what you tell me each night about them, how harsh they are with you? Are you sick of them or are you not, Malika? We have to do something, make a decision. Keep moving forward, despite everything in life. A café in the various weekly souks of this bled is not the future. I'll go to Indochina for a year, two years, maybe. No more. I keep telling you. It's a contract with the French. I've already signed. I can't go back on it. And they can't not respect the contract. No matter what people say, the French are reliable. I'm doing business with them. That's all. I don't see another path ahead of me, Malika. There is only the war. With the French. On the side of the French.

You like the French now, my husband Allal? You trust them? You've forgotten, apparently, how they invaded Morocco. The massacres. The murders. The pure hatred. Everywhere. Everywhere. I wasn't born yet, it's true, but I was told all about it, this past, the weapons, the planes in the sky that destroyed entire villages and *douars*.* Just as you were told, too. Did you forget?

---

* Small rural villages.

We don't exist for France, Allal. We are nothing for France. Just people ready to be colonized.

I am nothing here, with my parents. They control everything in my life. In my marriage. I give them most of what I earn at the café. You know this, Malika. I'm taking the risk. There is only the path of Indochina ahead of me. I've already signed the contract. I leave at the end of the month. In one week, I'll receive my military uniform.

All the love of this earth.

All the love that there is on this earth will never be able to console me. Nothing will help me turn the page, fully move on. I'll pretend in front of the others. I'll be another Malika. I am no longer me.

Allal, you are dead.

You followed roads that I will never know. You breathed the air of another country. You ate other foods. You saw other people, other landscapes, other skies. You entered into the hearts of people that I will never meet. You traveled to the depths of an existence that will be forever unknown to me.

You had formidable weapons with you. They taught you very quickly how to use them. You became another Allal. You fired without hesitation. So many times. In broad daylight. In deep darkness. And, one morning, they fired at you. That's what I imagine. That's what I see. Allal, over there. At the end of his life. Cruel Allal. Allal falling, falling. Allal on the ground. A body, so alone. He stops breathing. His heart stops beating. His eyes are still open. No one thinks to close them. What does he see?

You left for the war in the middle of the night, Allal. You had said that you didn't want to see my tears, the start of my new solitude.

Stay in bed, Malika. See you soon, Malika. Take care of yourself, Malika. Eat donuts and think of me, Malika.

I'm not crying. Don't worry, Allal. I'm not crying over you. I have no more tears left in me.

You didn't teach me how to forget you.

I should have, a few seconds after you left, stood up and gone to the door of the house. Opened it. Looked for you in the dark. Already gone. Already an invisible trace, a phantom, a spirit. Just a lingering scent. Reached my hand toward you. Toward the darkness. And faced the confirmation of this truth: no one can escape their destiny, their *mektoub*.

We are here. On this earth. And then suddenly, we are no longer here. It's as if we were never here.

Goodbye, Allal. Goodbye.

IN THE FIRST MONTH of our marriage, you brought me to the Ouzoud Falls. Do you remember, Allal?

You said: I'm going to show you my favorite place in the world. You might be afraid, Malika. You'll probably feel a bit dizzy. But I'll be there with you. I won't let go of your hand. Trust me.

We took the bus. It drove through the night. We arrived very early in the morning. It was still dark out. And then we walked for two hours.

It was winter.

By the Ouzoud Falls, there was snow everywhere. A big white carpet had covered the world. It was beyond beautiful. Beyond magical.

Eternal happiness exists. It is white.

I was seeing snow for the first time in my life. So much snow everywhere, everywhere. On the roads. On the fields. On the roofs of houses. On the trees and on the Atlas Mountains all around us, which I was also seeing for the first time.

You were offering me the world, Allal. Another side of the world.

When we arrived at the very top of the falls, you said: This is my gift to you, Malika. Look. Open your eyes and look. Open your heart and enter with me into all the details of this landscape. Ouzoud in the heart of winter. Give me your hand and look. Not many people know this place. If I die before you, come here and pray for me. Make the journey here alone and pray for me. When I die, I will be here, in this place, in this waterfall, between the sky and the earth.

I didn't pay attention to those words at the time. They only came back to me later, when, several months after you left for Indochina, we received the horrible news.

For now, I am with you, in the white silence of the world. You guide me. You show me the path. I am afraid. I am cold. I feel a bit dizzy staring at all this falling water, incredibly loud and incredibly deafening. But I want to see everything. I am far from everything life had planned for me. Here, without uttering the words, you say to me: *Kanbrik,* Malika. I love you, Malika. *Nti dyali,* Malika. You are mine, Malika. I hear you. I do not answer you. We continue our descent.

Life can stop here for me, on this path. Death can come. I accept it.

I know deeply that this opening to the world, this opening between you and me, will not reappear in the future.

We are below the falls now. So small, so crushed by the immense force of the water that reaches us, enters us, wrecks and resurrects everything in us. We are very cold, very hungry, you and I. Our teeth chatter. But we stay there. Captivated, in the literal sense of the word. Happy. Thrilled. Obeying an energy greater than us. Facing a truth that grasps us and surpasses us.

We must absolutely not resist this grandeur and this beauty. Just be here. Accept being nothing but an insignificant detail.

Allal and Malika. Surrounded by love. The only beings in the world.

It is only us in Ouzoud. Only us. Very close. And silent.

I take a few steps away from you, Allal. I lift my head to the sky. I murmur: Thank you. Thank you. Thank you.

Suddenly, we hear the hellish noise of a machine. A few seconds later, the earth begins to shake.

Is it an earthquake, Allal?

No.

Is it a volcano erupting?

Not that either.

What then? What?

In the sky, a flying machine appears.

It's a helicopter, you say, Allal.

I almost can't believe it. And yet it's there, that helicopter, just above us. In the void. Flying. Flying. We can even see the five or six French soldiers who are inside. One of them dangles his feet in the air. I can't believe it. A flying machine and a soldier dangling his feet in the air. He's not at all afraid. Me, I'm terrified. I see the soldier as something not human, not of this world, of our world. Something that heralds the end of the world.

The helicopter will destroy everything, won't it, Allal? They're going to kill us?

You don't answer. You keep your eyes on the machine's trajectory.

I crouch down. I place my hands over my eyes. This isn't how I imagined I would die. I don't want to look.

The hellish sound grows distant, little by little.

I stand up. The helicopter is still in the sky, still flying through the void, but far from us now. I am not reassured, however. I look at you, Allal. Say something. Take me in your arms.

Those French soldiers are probably looking for members of the Resistance who've escaped from the Béni Mellal prison.

To kill them?

They won't hesitate. Or else they're heading to a rebel village to punish its residents.

Punish them how, Allal?

Kill them, Malika. All of them. The whole village. It wouldn't be the first time.

We were still at the foot of the Ouzoud Falls, but its beauty and its magic suddenly seemed so far away from us. It was as though that helicopter were chasing us out of paradise. And that was exactly what it was doing. It removed us from what was pulsing strongly within us, this glacial place, and around us, that magical waterfall.

This isn't for you, the Ouzoud Falls. You don't deserve to be here, amidst all these riches. What are you doing here? Ouzoud is not for you.

Fear, still and terrifying, replaces our amazement. If the soldiers kill us, no one will know, not our families and not our douar.

This is the end.

The helicopter in the sky turns around. It comes back. It heads for us. For us.

This is the end, Malika.

This is the end, Allal?

They must have spotted us because of your blue *djellaba**
and my black djellaba. In this snow-covered landscape, we stand out. Blue and black.

The helicopter is approaching, Allal. I see the soldier and his feet dangling in the void. I see his weapon. He's pointing it at us. Should I start reciting the *chahada*** before we die? Let's do it, Allal, the two of us at the same time.

No, Malika. Wait. Wait. I have an idea. Put your hands in the air. Go on. Like me. Hands in the air. That way, they'll

---

* A loose, long garment with sleeves and a hood.
** The Islamic declaration of faith.

see that we're not criminals, not rebels, not Resistance fighters. Hands in the air, Malika. Don't look at me like that. Do what I tell you. You're right, the soldier is pointing his gun at us.

He's going to kill us. He's going to kill us.

The helicopter flies lower now. Then, hovering in the air, it stops moving. The propellers continue to spin rapidly and cause an extraordinary commotion, in us and around us. But that machine remains suspended in the air. It doesn't fall. It doesn't fall. I don't understand.

Three other soldiers have joined the one who still has his feet dangling in the void. One of them must be Moroccan. He looks like us. He could be our cousin.

This cousin takes a loudspeaker and shouts, in Arabic:

Take off your hoods! Show your faces!

We do so immediately. And then we put our hands back up in the air.

The four soldiers stare at us for a long time without saying anything. A minute, perhaps. A minute in hell. Ouzoud is no longer a place in the heart of winter. No. It's an inferno and a tornado at the same time. Where are we exactly? And that flying machine, is it real? Is it really there in front of us? And those soldiers staring at us, are they like us, human beings made like us? I feel no connection to them. Even the Moroccan soldier serving the French has stopped resembling us. He is not our cousin anymore.

Allal and I, we are nothing. We keep our hands in the air. We don't lower our eyes. We look at this thing in front of us. We are not afraid. It's something other than fear, what we feel.

The helicopter has eyes. A mouth. Two wheels like two little feet. Very long arms. But it's not from here, not from this planet. It's not possible. Who could have invented such a thing?

The helicopter dominates everything. It is stronger and more powerful than everything that exists around us. Even the Ouzoud Falls cannot compete.

The helicopter is like an angry god. An enraged god. A god born in hell. A god that is not Allah.

I turn my head toward you, Allal. This might be the last time I see you. You are beautiful. You are mine. I am yours. This is certain.

Look straight ahead, Malika. Otherwise, they'll shoot us.

I'm about to turn when suddenly I notice that the bottoms of your yellow pants are wet.

You pissed yourself, Allal. I should have done the same. Piss. Piss.

I do it.

Urine flows from me rapidly. An incredibly violent stream that courses through my *sirwal*,* my caftan, my djellaba, and pools on the ground.

My piss joins your piss, Allal.

Look straight ahead, Malika. Do what I tell you.

The helicopter moves a bit closer to us.

You can recite the chahada now, Malika. I'll do the same.

This is the end, Allal.

Yes, Malika. This is the end.

I am your woman, Allal.

I am your man, Malika.

The helicopter begins to climb back up slowly. High. Higher and higher in the sky. We watch it go, without understanding.

The helicopter grows distant. It crosses the valley ahead of us. It disappears behind the mountains.

We keep our hands in the air. You never know.

Ouzoud is silent again, peaceful, glacial, beautiful, so beautiful. But it doesn't move us at all, Allal and I. We are on the verge of tears. We can't cry. We lower our hands. Without saying anything, we turn toward the falls. We listen to the water running, falling. Smashing. Pulverizing. Again. Again and again.

---

* Loose-fitting pants.

It does us a world of good.

We come back to life, to ourselves, bit by bit. But we are unable to speak.

The Ouzoud Falls lure us, call us.

We must now drink some of its water.

You take my hand, Allal. We walk toward the falls. We are neither cold nor angry. We are thirsty. Just thirsty.

Together, we will live and we will forget the shock that we have just experienced. Endured.

That is the only solution. Hope that one day we will forget.

YOUR FRIEND MERZOUGUE HAS become a shadow of himself. He doesn't want to see me anymore. He says that when he sees me, he sees only you.

He's delirious, he says strange things.

My head, Malika. My head can't take it anymore. It's so loud in my head. Allal isn't dead. He's just hiding. He will return, reappear, revive. Get away from me, Malika. Don't come around and remind me of the part of me I'll never be able to erase: Allal who is gone now. Go, go far away from me. I know that it's because of you, all this. Money. Money. Ever since he married you, that was all he talked about. Before you, with me, he didn't need money. We didn't need anything. People saw us passing in the streets, walking in the fields, working in the souks, and they said: Allal and Merzougue, there they are, inseparable. Merzougue and Allal. It didn't bother anyone. It wasn't anyone's business but ours. They knew. They saw. And they kept quiet. Then you showed up, Malika. I saw your game, your ruse from the start. What you were doing in the souk to bewitch and dis-orient Allal. Your shameless dances. You were perfect, Malika. Perfectly suited to fill Allal's eyes and heart with fog. Bravo. I'll kill you, Malika. Even before he went over there, to Indochina, to give his body and soul to France, it was here, in our bled, that the disaster began. The disaster that was Malika and the family he had to build with her. And for that, he had to find money. Become a killer to earn money. I'm about to burst, overflow, explode. My head. My head . . .

I just want to sleep, Malika. I just want to get some sleep. Forget all this pain and this absence, if that's even possible. Take me to the mausoleum of Saint Moulay Brahim. He'll calm me down, Moulay Brahim. He'll understand me, return Allal to me. He still remembers the two of us, Moulay Brahim. Allal and Merzougue. It was there, in his mausoleum, that we would meet. It was there that we would touch each other. It was there that we would cross the boundaries, the limits.

Our first time was in that mausoleum, Malika. We were two free young boys. Our last time too, just before Indochina.

Moulay Brahim is not like the other saints. He understands, he understands, he hears, he hears. Take me, Malika, guide me to his *zaouïa*, to his tomb.

What will they do to me now that Allal is gone? They'll destroy me, throw rocks at me, kill me, cut my body up into a thousand pieces and throw them to the dogs. Won't they? My protector has vanished. My brother, my love, is in heaven. He doesn't even have a grave here. He will never have a grave among us. What a tragedy . . .

I'm so afraid, Malika. Come, Malika. Come close to me. Hold my head in your hands. I forgive you, Malika.

Moulay Brahim is this way. Let's go there, Malika. Hold me, carry me. I can't take it anymore.

France is still there. France will send us all to die in Indochina.

Moulay Brahim, Malika. Moulay Brahim. Stay with me, Malika. Don't leave. We'll sleep side by side now. Just you and me.

IT'S LIKE THIS EVERY day. Merzougue calls me. I go to him and I listen.

Merzougue is all I have left. The unruly voice of Merzougue. The justice and injustice of Merzougue. And his saint, our Saint Moulay Brahim. That's where I have to renegotiate the future, that's where I'll be able to hide. Among other pilgrims, alongside Merzougue, lie down on the ground, close my eyes, nestle myself in your arms, Allal, picture them and let me be taken by them.

Later, wake up Merzougue.

Allal is here, Merzougue. He's here. His spirit. Listen. Listen. He's breathing. Do you hear him? Do you recognize him? Speak. It's Allal. Speak to him, Merzougue. He's listening.

Allal's spirit has made the voyage from over there, Indochina, where his body died, all the way here: the mausoleum of Saint Moulay Brahim. Please, Merzougue. Get up. Don't go back to sleep. We'll find a solution. Allal's parents can't reject us like this, as easily as this. Take everything from us and throw us in the street like sick dogs.

Our Saint Moulay Brahim is here for this too, for the people of this country like you and me, we who are lost, flattened, amputated from the Tree of Life.

The others don't exist anymore, Merzougue. There is only Moulay Brahim's tomb, where we sleep and hope. There is only you, you who are much better than all the others, I know that now. Let them spew their venom and their judgments. I, Malika, know who you are, and even if you don't love me, I love you. I love you and I need you.

Sit up. Let Allal return through you, let him make the spiritual journey from over there to here. Open your eyes, Merzougue. You, you have the baraka, the blessing necessary for our Allal to carry out this journey and this dream. You, you have the spirits, you have the jinns in you. They will help you to help our Allal.

Even dead, Allal is still alone over there, in Indochina, in that country we will never know. A lone body in a lone grave.

A non-Muslim grave.

Allal must come back here. His body must find its first land again. Do you hear me, Merzougue? Allal must be buried here. Even if it's symbolic, we must do everything to bring back his body. Even if you are not convinced, follow me in the realization of this dream. Even if it's sorcery, we have to see it through.

Rescue Allal from his solitude over there.

Please, Merzougue, wake up and let him make the impossible voyage through your body. Moulay Brahim is with us.

It's night, Merzougue. Tell Allal to come. To take the path. We're waiting for him here, in Moulay Brahim's mausoleum, which he knows very well. Tell him that we'll wait the whole night. Tell him that we won't cry. We are strong. We are happy. We will reunite.

We love him, Allal. Still and always.

By the end of the night, Allal will have a grave here. His Muslim grave with us, next to us, for us.

We will do this incredible thing. We will perform this miracle.

ALL THE LOVE THAT there is on this earth will not be enough.

I will never forgive your parents, Allal. My heart is forever black against them. As soon as they had the confirmation that they would receive the money from France within two months, the compensation for your death, Allal, they sprang into action. They had made their decision a long time ago.

Someone came to tell them that they had to go to the city of Marrakech. The French police had something to offer them.

Your parents, Allal, did not hesitate. They weren't afraid of France, not at all. I was shocked. Normally, no one wants to have anything to do with the police, who can send you to the other side of the sun in an instant. But not them. Not your mother. Not your father. Not your two brothers.

They put on their best clothes. As though they were going to a wedding. And they took the bus to Marrakech.

France awaited them. France would compensate them. It was a day of celebration.

The money for your death. The price of your death, Allal. You killed for France, Allal. You are a hero. A man who kills is a real man. Isn't he?

Some in the bled used to mock you. They said that you were Merzougue's husband. The money from France made them all change their minds. Now they're quiet. They forgot so quickly.

You're an important man. You're a hero, Allal. Do you hear me? Are you happy? France made it happen. You're a hero. A man, a hero. And on top of it, you made your family rich by your death. What a good son he was, our Allal! Kindness incarnate and generosity itself.

Everything was turned upside down after your death. The winds began to blow from everywhere and in every direction. They entered us, me, and destroyed everything in us.

Everything is dark. Life isn't life anymore.

Your parents said to me:

Malika, you knew Allal for barely two years. You were his wife for barely two years. That's not long.

It's basically nothing! your mother shouted.

Nothing, nothing at all, your father added.

Your two brothers were quiet. They didn't agree with this condemnation, this injustice, I saw it, but they knew that it wasn't in their interest to speak, to defend me. They went mute.

Your mother, Allal. Your mother. A woman, like me, who was the first to turn her back on me. She was the leader, she pushed them not to falter, to see it through.

We're not sharing the money from France with that Malika. She's a stranger, that Malika. Nothing but a little girl, that Malika. We'll do with her what we want, manipulate her how we want. Maybe we'll give her a thousand dirhams, that's all, nothing more. A thousand dirhams, that's a lot, that's huge. She should consider herself very fortunate. A thousand dirhams. Nothing more. You hear that, Malika? You won't get any more.

Don't respond, it's not necessary.

Your mother, Allal, who had told my father the day when we signed the marriage contract: I know Malika lost her mother at a very young age. From now on, she will be my daughter. She is my daughter. Do you remember, Allal, those falsely tender words?

My daughter Malika, she said. God is my witness, she swore.

I became a maid in your home. A slave for your mother. That was what it meant to be your mother's daughter. Wash the dirty clothes, Malika. Clean the house again, Malika, it's not clean enough. You only have an hour to grind the wheat, Malika, understand? You didn't do a good job with the cooking today, Malika. It's bad. Are you still sleeping, Malika? It's already six in the morning. Get up, get up, go milk the cow and then make the crêpes for breakfast. Don't take a nap, Malika, you'll develop bad habits. How lazy she is, really, that Malika! Our son has rotten luck. Truly.

You said nothing to your mother, Allal. And your father acted as though he saw nothing, as though it were none of his business.

God had sent you the daughter your parents never had. So let her live out a girl's destiny. There's nothing to be done. The kitchen's over there. The well to fetch the water is behind the house. And the basin to wash the dirty laundry each day is on the terrace.

A thousand dirhams. Nothing more. You won't get any more, they told me. Allal is dead now. Dead several months already. You can leave. We don't need you anymore. Luckily for you, you didn't have children with him. Go on.

You are free, Malika.

Your mother's final words, before slamming the door of her house behind me, still turn in my head: A thousand dirhams—really, Malika. You're lucky, Malika. We were too kind to you.

Allal. Allal. Allal. I will love you forever despite your silence and your submission to your parents. I love you. I miss you. Where are you? Are you on the way? Keep going. Keep going. Merzougue is ready to receive your body through his body. Keep going through the night, Allal. Keep going. Even dead, come back to us. Come back to me.

I did what I could to convince you not to follow your parents' advice. They're the ones who urged you to fight in Indochina. You hesitated. They convinced you. They forced you to sign the contract. You were afraid of France. Like me, you hadn't forgotten the helicopter and the French soldiers at the Ouzoud Falls. They wanted to kill us. Kill us when we had just barely begun to live in the illusion of happiness. Why didn't they do it? Like me, you knew what the French were capable of. How could you change your mind and align yourself with them? How? I asked you that question a hundred times. No use. You had nothing to say. Your parents mattered much more than me. Children don't ever belong to themselves, where we're from. They belong to their parents and their grandparents. Who can do with them what they like. Beat them. Exploit them. Rape them. Insult them. Marry them off to whomever they want. Make them get divorced. I knew all that long before I met you, Allal. But to see you so small before your parents, paralyzed before your parents, a child again before your parents, that was beyond shocking. The end of innocence. The disappearance of the final trace of innocence in me.

Money. Money. Money. That was all your parents talked

about. And they wouldn't hesitate to sacrifice a son for it. Sacrifice Allal. Money. France's money.

You have brought me onto the terrace, Allal. It's night. Everyone is asleep in the house. You have something to tell me. There's still hope. We'll both remember what we experienced on the Ouzoud Falls and make a decision. Is that it? Is that it, Allal?

Answer me. I don't want to become a mean woman, too. A harsh, cold, authoritarian woman. Like your mother. If you leave, Allal, that's what will happen to me. I'll change. My heart will turn to stone. Speak, Allal. Tell me that you'll stay. Tell me that you're still the man I saw in the café, in the souk. You are life itself, I see it in your eyes while I dance for you in front of everyone. I don't want to become an adult like the people here. I don't want to become your mother, or your father, and especially not my own father. If growing up means becoming a shameless coward, then I want to stay young and a slave until the end. I found you, Allal. That's enough for me. It's a miracle. You're a man. You have balls and a full, beautiful beard. You can say no. You will say no to your parents. You will shed the fear they imposed on you. Shed the forced respect. Shed the submission. You are a man. A man. How many times do I have to say it? Tell me. Money isn't everything in life. Say no. No. No.

You're lying on the terrace floor, Allal. I see you.

Your eyes are fixed on the sky. What should I make of this? What should I do, what should I do with myself?

I keep staring at you. Just for a moment. I won't let myself be softened by that gentleness you exude. Be firm, Malika. Be mean. Be a man in Allal's stead. Force him to stay. Enter his head and fill it with your sorcery and magical songs.

I don't do any of that. I lie down next to you. On the ground like you. Right next to you. And your body. Right next to your breath. Your heart. And your silence.

You won't say anything. It's too late. You are the well-raised son of your parents. The son crushed by your parents. I don't love you anymore. I detest you. I hate you. I was wrong. I am disappointed.

The silence stretches between us.

I abandon my anger. It's no longer useful to me. I emerge from my fictitious hatred for you.

We both stare at the sky. The black of the sky. The stars of the sky. There is really nothing left to say.

No one is free in this life. No one. No one. That's what your silence says to me.

They are my parents. They are my parents. I can't go against their wishes. I can't, Malika.

Did you say those words? Yes? No?

I turn to face you. I call you. You turn to face me. Our eyes meet. I must not cry. No, Allal, I won't make things easy for you. I endure the injustice of this world like you and much more than you. I see what will happen to you if you choose France. I say nothing. I stare deep into your eyes. Through your eyes, I can stay in love a little longer. The love that is Allal. Present. Already absent. Already a memory.

Mehdi Ben Barka* will save Morocco.

You say these very strange words. I think you're delirious. You don't know where you are anymore, nor what you're saying.

Who is Mehdi Ben Barka?

My question snaps you out of your reverie. You're surprised. You smile.

What? You don't know Mehdi Ben Barka, France's number one enemy in Morocco?

You're serious. You're not delirious at all, Allal. I have the impression that you're talking about a legend, a story from

---

* Moroccan nationalist and anti-imperialist, head of the National Union of Popular Forces (UNPF); assassinated in 1965 at the age of forty-five, his body was never recovered.

another century, another time, when Morocco was only Morocco. Bled Makhzen. Bled Siba. Us and only us. Something we didn't know but that continues to live in us, despite all the changes the French make each day in Morocco. Mehdi Ben Barka comes from this world? The first world? Mehdi Ben Barka is the first man?

Mehdi Ben Barka is like us, Malika. He is one of the masses, too. He fights for the masses. And he used the French educational system to progress, to learn, to complete advanced studies, become as good as the French, better than the French at their language and their logic. And, during all those years, he never forgot his origins or the Moroccan people waiting to be liberated. He will liberate us one day, Ssi Ben Barka. He is the leader of this country. The true leader. He's like us. He loves us. He truly thinks of us. He has big ideas in his head. He is a man of heart and mind.

You're delirious again, Allal, I think. You're leaving to kill in Indochina, and the night before you go you're talking to me about a Moroccan hero who fights against France. I don't understand it at all. It's completely contradictory. But it's moving, very moving, to see you this way, emotional, passionate, wrapped up in a hope bigger than you and me. It's deeply touching to see you return to your natural state. A fire resurrects you. You have so many things to say about this Mehdi Ben Barka. You want to keep telling me at all costs. Your eyes look at me and dream of him. I don't tell you what I think. My doubts. I listen to you. You're still mine. I listen to everything you say. True or not, crazy or not, it doesn't matter. You are here. You touch my hand and continue to speak. You want to convince me at all costs, to convert me to this religion invented by this man.

In the beginning, Mehdi would stand outside, against a wall of the French school in Rabat that his older brother attended. At the time, the French accepted only one child per family into their schools. Mehdi would stand right next to the classroom window and follow the lessons. He did that for weeks, months. He didn't give up. It was difficult and humiliating, but he was spurred by something bigger than himself. He wanted to be like his older brother. Go where his older brother went each day. He was so young. Perhaps he was just jealous of his brother. But this jealousy served as a driving force, as motivation. Wake up in the morning. Stand by the window of his older brother's classroom. Listen. Learn. Without their permission. Imagine himself in his brother's place, alongside him. Imagine himself answering the French teacher's questions. Shine. Win. That's what ended up happening, Malika. Believe it or not. They say that, one day, the teacher asked a question of one of his students. None of them knew the answer. So then Mehdi stands up, on the other side of the window, and he has the answer. The answer in French. The right answer in French. A small Moroccan child dressed in a djellaba stands up and affirms his presence, imposes his answer, reveals his intelligence and his patience. The teacher is enthralled, both by the perfect answer and by this child of the masses who, from the outside, has done everything to carve out a place for himself. Mehdi has commanded fate. Has written his mektoub. The French teacher cannot stand before or against mektoub, which could then turn against him. The teacher asks the child to enter the classroom. Mehdi enters. Through the window. Through the window, Malika. He jumps. He approaches the teacher. The teacher asks him questions in French. Mehdi answers in French. Mehdi, who looks like a poor street urchin in his djellaba, speaks better French than all the other students, has answers to all the teacher's questions. All of them. He knows everything, little Mehdi. Everything is there, already in place. And the teacher has nothing else to do but put himself in service of destiny, in service of that intelligence. It's the teacher's day of glory. He has discovered Mehdi Ben Barka. And he will do everything to get him officially enrolled in the French school of Rabat. He brings Mehdi with him to the principal's office. He presents Mehdi to him. He asks Mehdi to leave the office and wait for him outside. Little Mehdi obeys. He waits. He smiles, on the inside. He doesn't sit in one of the chairs in the hallway. He knows that he shouldn't do that. He remains standing. He remains focused. The French school administrators who find him there, standing against the wall, look at him with surprise and poorly veiled contempt. But he, Mehdi, already knows that he has won. He has forced all their hands. He doesn't react to their unjust stares. He remains dignified. A young, clever Rabati child, very clever, who knows how to behave there, in this extraordinary situation. He is standing before the office of the French principal of the French school. He behaves like a gentleman. Mehdi doesn't come from the Moroccan bourgeoisie, but his mother, Fatouma, raised him well. He waits there. For a long time. Calm. Confident. In the hallway. He is sure of himself. But he remains modest.

The teacher comes out of his office. He smiles. Success. Immediately he brings little Mehdi to the secretary's office to begin his enrollment. Write this name: Mehdi Ben Barka. He asks the child to return the next day with his father. What's his father's name? Ahmed Ben M'Hammed Ben Barka. The teacher is impressed. By this name and by Mehdi's precision. He knows where he comes from, this little Mehdi. He already knows everything. Nothing will be easy of course, but it's clear that he's not afraid of a fight.

His father didn't believe Mehdi. But he went with him to the school the next day. The gates of heaven have opened before you, my son. Not only the gates of heaven, my father, Mehdi answered.

Now I see why you're telling me all this, Allal.

I am not Mehdi Ben Barka, Malika. But Mehdi Ben Barka is now in you as he is in me. I must tell you about him. About what he will bring. He went very far. He earned all his degrees. He became a mathematics professor. They say that not so long ago, he was the teacher of Prince Hassan, the son of Sultan Ben Mohammed. You see how far Mehdi went. From the classroom window of the French school in Rabat straight to the Holy of Holies. But being among them never intimidated him. Neither the French, nor the royal family, nor the bourgeoisie managed to tame him, to turn him into a gentle Moroccan who looked like them and spoke their sophisticated language. They didn't succeed in making him forget the poor and abandoned Moroccans. The Morocco waiting to be liberated. Ben Barka is more than a leader. More than a king. More than a general. He's a man who's one of us, who thinks of us, who works for us. You have to know this, Malika.

I leave tomorrow for Indochina. For money, Malika. For my parents, Malika. For you, Malika. I will return. I promise you. I swear to you. I will return and we will speak again of Mehdi Ben Barka. I will return and bring you to Rabat, the city of Mehdi Ben Barka. I will return. Do you hear me? Don't be too angry at me, please. This is my destiny. My destiny. Indochina. And you, you will wait for me. Tell me that you will wait for me.

You will return, Allal. I know so. I hope so.

Mehdi Ben Barka will do here what I will never be able to do.

Don't judge yourself, Allal.

Now you know Mehdi Ben Barka.

I know him and I love him.

Suddenly you go quiet, Allal. You have nothing more to say. Nor do I. We look at each other. And that's it.

The tears begin to flow from your eyes. I watch them cross the different parts of your face. You don't wipe them away. You're not ashamed. The tears flow. Flow. It's not sad. It's beautiful. It's a gift. A pact among you, Mehdi Ben Barka, and me.

I AM BARELY TWENTY years old.

Your mother threw me out and slammed the door behind me.

Where will I go now? To my father's house? His second wife and his three daughters detest me. Go there anyway, Malika, try your luck. Perhaps if you show them the thousand dirhams that Allal's mother gave you they will be kind. Go on. Money changes everything. Go on.

My father wasn't home. He'd gone to Azilal to sell the harvest.

His wife and daughters hadn't changed. Not at all. Black hearts, black eyes. That's what they were and always would be.

Your father will be gone for at least a month, Malika. What do you want with him? You want to spend the night here with us? One night, just one night. No more than one night.

I am barely twenty years old.

In this countryside and in this bled, without you, Allal, where else can I go? Where can I find my bearings? Where can I laugh so as not to cry?

I gave the thousand dirhams to my father's wife and I left. I didn't want that money. It reeked of death.

They killed you. You're dead, Allal. And you don't even have a grave here. It's as if you never existed among us.

Merzougue came back to my mind as I was wandering aimlessly. I must find him. And with him, at night, I must dig a grave for you. At last.

Allal's grave.

There. I've found a mission. Something to do. A task to accomplish. What a wife must do for her husband.

I am barely twenty years old.

I've worn white, the color of mourning, for several months now.

A widow at not even twenty years old.

Merzougue sleeps ever since you left for Indochina, Allal. He doesn't wake up anymore. What for?! To meet whom? See what?

Merzougue has given up entirely.

I found him in the mausoleum of our Saint Sidi Moulay Brahim. I sat down next to him. And I waited.

When he woke up, I gave him the donut with sugar that I had bought specially for him.

He ate. Slowly.

I spoke to him.

Allal stayed with you, Merzougue, when I arrived in his life. He didn't throw you out. If only for that, this act of absolute, rare loyalty, you must get up and help me to perform this miracle: bring back Allal's dead body from so far away. Do this impossible and magical thing tonight. Here. In this mausoleum. Bring him back here, defying all the laws of nature. And tomorrow morning, very early, just before sunrise, bury him. At last. Give him a funeral. At last. What Allal's own parents refused him, we, you and me, the survivors, we will do.

The body, visible and invisible.

Thanks to you, Merzougue.

They can't see him, the others. We are the only ones in on this secret, this great miracle. We will defy every law.

Allal will be here. In Indochina an hour ago. Before us, in Béni Mellal, now.

We will pray softly as we wash his body. We will sing beautifully when we place him in the beautiful shroud.

Together we will place him in his final home, his grave. No matter that religion forbids me as a woman from witnessing and participating in this ceremony. Allah is magnanimous. He will understand. He will not condemn me. I will do what the men did not want to do for Allal. They have stopped thinking of him. He doesn't exist for them anymore. That's not the case for me. Or for you.

A grave. A grave. That's our duty, Merzougue. Get up. Open yourself, let Allal come, take you, possess you, live through you and then die. Get up, get up. No one will stop us. Night is with us. France and its people in Morocco are asleep. This is the time to try this indispensable thing without which we will not be able to keep on living. Allal's parents will soon be rich, but without us. We don't want the shameful money they received from France. They sold Allal. They received their price. And now they will be cursed for a long time. We don't want anything more to do with them. From a distance, we will witness their glory and their fall. Nothing is ever forgotten.

We will bury Allal, Merzougue. We will not put his name on his grave. We will tell no one that it's his grave. No one, you hear me?

ALLAL. ALLAL. YOU'RE HERE. You have arrived. I smell your scent. I breathe your air. You're here. Merzougue's heart is your heart. Merzougue's body is your body. I've missed you, so much, so much. I don't eat donuts with sugar anymore. I don't dance anymore. I don't dream anymore. The world after you has shown me its true face, its red eyes, harsh and merciless. I thought that I was intelligent, that the suffering of childhood had transformed me into a woman who wasn't afraid of anything. I was so wrong. My cunning turned out to be no danger to them. My intelligence couldn't save me. I saw evil after you, Allal. I saw hell. They threw me out. I'm nothing without you, Allal. The curtain has been lifted. And what's behind it is not beautiful.

I'm barely twenty years old. So young. So old.

Two years ago, you were still sleeping next to me. For me. The others could say what they wanted, you were mine. I had succeeded in my mission.

God loved me, at that moment.

You are not a traitor, Allal. You are not a traitor. Give me your hand. Let me breathe you in from up close. Let me place my head on your thighs and close my eyes for a moment. Your thighs, Allal. The living memory of your thighs.

They took the money from France, Allal. And they will forget you.

You are dead, Allal. You have returned. Merzougue and I, we see you. We imagine you. We see you. We will bury you.

It's dark. The sun will rise. Now we must dig the grave.

The two of us place you in the dirt, all the way at the bottom. And we wait for the sky to turn slightly pink, slightly blue.

There's the sun, Malika.

Say a prayer, Merzougue. Say what you know of the Koran. With love, Merzougue. Say it with love.

We covered your visible and invisible body with dirt.

Now you have a grave, Allal.

I poured orange-blossom water onto it. Merzougue repeated verses from the Koran. Crying. Then he was quiet.

What will happen to us now?

I am barely twenty years old, Merzougue.

I had only Allal, Malika.

Merzougue lay down next to the grave. And he embraced it.

Without hesitation, I did the same.

You are between us, Allal. A grave for us. A past that will never die on a colonized land where we are rejected, banished, condemned to wander for eternity and to start over endlessly.

I am barely twenty years old, Allal. And already everything is over.

2

Rabat

*

THEY WERE RIGHT, MY CHILDREN. THAT woman is white, so white. It's incomprehensible, how does she manage to be so white? It's not skin that she has, no, it's milk. My mouth is watering. Despite myself, I want to lick her. Walk right up to her and, without saying a word, lick her skin. Taste her skin very slowly. Drink that milk. It's impossible, that skin, especially here in Rabat, especially now, in the middle of August. I'm drenched in sweat, my whole body is dripping. Rivers and rivers of sweat. I can't take it anymore. I feel as if I'm going to faint. But she, who is not even from this country, is not sweating. She really isn't sweating. I stare and stare at her. I can't believe it. She walked the same path as me up to this monument, the Chellah ruins, and there's not a drop of sweat visible on her. What's her secret? It's honestly unfair. To be so white, so beautiful without makeup, and tolerate the blazing sun of Morocco so effortlessly. I was born and have always lived here, and yet I have no solution. The sun doesn't love me. It strikes me, splits my head open with migraines day and night, throws me into an ocean of cold and hot sweats. Only eucalyptus leaves help me recover slightly. I crush them in the mortar and place them on my forehead. A bit of coolness. A bit of coldness across my entire head. A bit of springtime in the middle of summer. But I made a mistake: I forgot to cut a few branches from the eucalyptus trees that lined the path. Here, at the entrance to the Chellah ruins, there are no trees.

There is only her. White. Fresh. Well dressed.

There is only her and her milky skin.

She smiles. Why is she smiling? I can't return her smile. I have to remain strong, the strongest. I am not gentle Malika. I am not the Arab woman she thinks I am. I will not smile.

My name is Monique, she says.

She keeps smiling. That's her strategy in life. Always smile. Well, that won't work with me. I won't smile at her. I'm not kind, I'm mean. I'm intractable. I can't be bought. In any case, not with little smiles from another world.

No.

My name is Monique, she repeats.

I know her name is Monique. Why does she keep saying it?

Ana smiti Monique.

In Arabic this time. She really has no shame. She speaks in Arabic. She has no right. Well, it won't impress me. Not at all. Why does she speak Arabic like us? To bond with us? Know us better? I have my doubts.

She opens her mouth and utters words in Moroccan Arabic. Ana smiti Monique.

Monique. Monique. All right, all right. I know your name.

Monique, it comes from *monika*. A doll.

This Monique is no doll. I know that too, and have for at least two months now. She's the complete opposite. She's intelligent. She charges forward, she attacks. She never asks for permission.

Even so, she seems ridiculous when she speaks Moroccan.

I sense that she's going to tell me now that my name is Malika. She knows my first name already. That's what she does. She has no shame. She looks me straight in the eyes, smiles, acts innocent, naive, and she says Moroccan words. She says my first name once. Malika. Then twice in a row: Malika. Malika. I have no idea why.

It bothers me.

I look her straight in the eyes and still don't smile. I didn't come all this way, I didn't endure the heatwave of this road all the way to Chellah to buddy up to this Monique. I will never be your friend. I came here for other reasons. She knows this and acts as though, for now, this isn't the most important thing. She wants to set the rules of the game. Act like the French mistress? Mistress, but kind. Mistress, and sweet. Mistress from head to toe, but look how I'm not sweating, even in the middle of summer, look how fresh I am, how good I smell, as fragrant as vetiver, how elegant I am, how beautiful I am, how white I am, and so on and so forth.

I'm not impressed. I won't let myself be dominated so easily. No. No. He's dead and buried, the one who holds the key to my heart. Dead. Dead. Allal. I have no more master.

How can I make Monique understand this? How can I force her to look at me differently?

Make her stop smiling. Make her stop speaking Moroccan. It doesn't suit her. Make her stop acting as if she's benevolent toward us. Make her stop. We don't need her pity, definitely not her understanding. Make her lower her gaze and even her head. That way, I can devour her with my eyes, at last. Make her drop the mask of modern French woman who is so touched by the simplicity of Moroccan life. Colonization has been over for almost a decade now. Why does she insist on staying here? What is she doing in Rabat anyway? I know through my husband Mohammed that she was born in Casablanca in the thirties and that she lived there until she was ten. And, of course, she could never forget Morocco, the beauty of Morocco, the sky of Morocco, the light of Morocco. And the poverty of Moroccans, does she remember that? Of course she remembers it, and that's why she came back here, with her husband and their children. She wants to show them just how incredible this poor country is. Incredible.

Yes: Morocco is incredible. In-cre-di-ble.

Since we arrived in Rabat, thanks to the job my husband managed to find at the National Library, not a week goes by without someone telling me a supposedly touching story about the great beauty of Morocco.

Since I arrived in Rabat, every day I'm shocked. I thought the French left Morocco in 1956. But no. Not at all. They're still here, very much so. They live in villas in the nice neighborhoods of Rabat: Hassan. Agdal. Les Orangers. They're at home here. And even when they leave, they end up returning. They can't forget about Morocco. They can't live without Morocco. Nostalgia for Morocco, they say.

I refuse to enter into the logic of that nostalgia.

Monique lives in a very beautiful villa in the Orangers neighborhood. Her. Her husband. And their two boys. She has everything. What more could she want?

She has no daughter. Ah! That's what she's missing. A little girl.

Poor Monique. How I pity her . . . But she's found a solution.

Monique wants to steal my daughter. My own daughter. Khadija. Who's barely fifteen years old. Khadija, the most beautiful of my girls, Monique wants to hire her as a maid. A little maid.

Khadija will be like my own daughter, she dared say to my husband Mohammed.

And he, an idiot, a happy fool, is all for it. Give her Khadija. She'll have a future with Monique. That's what we should do. It's a good thing for Khadija. Whether you like it or not, Malika, you have to think of what's best for Khadija. It's a big opportunity for her. To be among the French. Do you realize?

To work in a French home. That's the royal road. They're rich, Malika. Rich. I know it.

From one day to the next, that first name, Monique, was everywhere in my home, on every lip, in every dream.

My six daughters spoke of nothing but her. Monique is beautiful. Monique is elegant. Monique is bourgeois but kind. Monique has such white skin. It's unbelievable!

The whiteness of her skin completely fascinated my daughters. They were won over. Monique was the dream.

My daughters are already arguing over who will take Khadija's place, in case she were to change her mind for whatever reason.

IN THIS HISTORIC MONUMENT, the Chellah ruins, where I told Monique to meet me, we will clarify things, settle the score. Put it all on the table. All of it.

I'm not afraid of you, Monique. Fear left my heart once and for all when everyone turned their back on me in Béni Mellal. So stop smiling. Stop speaking Moroccan. Stop with this strategy: it won't work for you. I know what you did to Khadija. I know every detail.

I was at the hammam. It was my day. The day when, once per month, I drop everything, leave my family, and go alone to the hammam.

Monique chose that day to enter my home: the two tiny rooms that serve as our house in the garden of the National Library. In my absence. My home. And, without anyone stopping her, she planted in my daughters' heads ideas that are not ours, dreams that are not for us.

I wasn't there. What a disaster! I should never have gone to the hammam that day.

My husband Mohammed made mint tea. Mohammed, who

never, never steps foot in the kitchen to help me, prepared mint tea for Monique. A true miracle.

Then he introduced her to our children. The eldest son. The six girls. And allowed them to stay with her, next to her. To look at her. To start constructing a kind of pipe dream around her.

They all drank mint tea. In my home. Without me. They got to know each other. They said things. Decided things.

They all liked Monique. None of them saw the danger.

I'm ashamed. I'm ashamed. I'm ashamed. Why did I go to the hammam that day?

Monique knew I wasn't home and she entered anyway. People don't do that. It isn't done—enter a poor family's home to observe just how poor they are, so very poor. People don't enter a house with a husband in the absence of his wife. No. I take that as a form of humiliation. Who does this Monique think she is?

They showed her everything in our tiny two-room house for nine people. They exposed our private life to her. All of our privacy. She must have seen that we have nothing. We own nothing. *Ouallou,* zilch. How shameful! How shameful for me! But that's not my main concern. She shouldn't have entered in my absence. She should have given us notice so that we could prepare. That's the least she could have done. Mohammed thinks, of course, that I'm overreacting. Yes, we're poor. So what?

Monique drank the mint tea prepared in my teapot and from the glasses that we had to save up to buy nine of. They served her little cakes that I'd made myself, but not for her.

I'll never forgive Mohammed for doing all that. Putting our daughters on display like that. Presenting them to Monique as if they were in a slave market. The choice is yours, madame. Six girls in good health. Look, madame. Khadija, fifteen years old.

Rachida, fourteen. Latifa, twelve. Fatima, ten. Najat, eight. Rabiaa, six. Which do you like the most?

I'm ashamed. I'm ashamed. Ashamed of my imbecile husband who sees only a yard in front of him and speaks without knowing what he's saying.

Mohammed defends Monique:

This is an incredible opportunity, Malika. Monique chose Khadija. Khadija will actually be able to escape poverty. And we'll escape with her, at the same time. We'll all escape poverty. Monique will return to France in two years, when her husband's contract has ended, and she'll bring Khadija with them, over there. Don't fight this, Malika. This is Khadija's destiny. It's her mektoub. It's Allah who wants this for our Khadija. He sent Monique to our home. I didn't go looking for her. He's the one who put her in front of me, on my path. She used to come to the library all the time. She was often alone in the large reading room. I made her a coffee one day and brought it to her. She thanked me and asked my name. I'm Mohammed. I'm the *chaouche* in this library. What's a chaouche? I answered: I do everything they ask me to. I put away the books. I distribute the mail to the other government employees. I make them mint tea and coffee. I'm here for them, at their service. They like me a lot, the people here. They intervened so that management would offer me a place to stay. They succeeded. I live in the library's garden, in back, with my family. I'm the chaouche of the National Library.

Mohammed expected me to congratulate him when he told me this. To be proud of him.

You played the *meskine*, the poor wretch, in front of her, Mohammed, is that it? Did she shed a tear for you?

You're too harsh, Malika. Sometimes we have to let luck make its way to us. Let mercy shine down on us. We need it.

And for you, luck is this Monique?

Allah placed me on the same path as her.

Is she beautiful?

She's . . . otherworldly. She's like a dream . . .

I understand, Mohammed. I understand perfectly. I don't accept. I won't sell Khadija. Khadija's destiny is not to become a maid. I refuse this destiny. Khadija will never become Monique's maid.

You're going against Allah's will. You're being blasphemous, Malika. Think about it. Monique will bring Khadija to France with her later on. This is the dream of every poor person in Morocco: to go to France.

It's not Khadija's dream. Do you hear me, Mohammed? I don't want to be separated from my daughter, live far away from her. Know nothing about her or how she spends her days and her nights. She's my daughter, not just yours, Mohammed. I want to watch her grow up, become a woman, find her way. Here in Morocco, with us. Not over there, in France, a planet that I know absolutely nothing about. And don't give me that look. Yes, I'm stubborn. Yes, my heart is made of iron. As you've told me several times already. Starting in the first week of our marriage. You see, I haven't changed. The same woman that you married in Béni Mellal. Exactly the same. Intractable. You, Mohammed, you're too trusting of people. Anyone can eat your brain, easily. Luckily for you, you have me in your life. I keep watch. I keep watch over you and over us all. I have foresight. You should kiss my feet. Thank Allah day and night that you have a woman like me in your life. Khadija is the most beautiful of my daughters. Everyone turns around when she walks in the street, even in the halls of this library. She's a queen, that girl. Don't you see? She's from this country and will stay in this country. We are in the center of power here, in Rabat, in the center of Morocco. The National Library shares a wall with the Royal Palace. And, just on the other side of the street, is the ministry neighborhood. Do you understand? Do you see what I'm getting at? Khadija is beautiful, very beautiful. We're in the right place. Someone important among all the important men around us will end up taking a liking to her and come ask us for her hand. In a year. Two years. That's the path you don't see, Mohammed. An important man. A man from the Royal Palace, why not? A queen's destiny for Khadija. Look at her. She's perfect for this world of important men. And you, you see her just as a maid, a little fifteen-year-old maid in a French woman's home in Orangers. Wake up, Mohammed! What did this Monique do to you? And don't tell me that you're the man of the house and already gave Monique your word. Don't make me laugh.

I couldn't convince Mohammed. Even all the sex he wanted didn't get me anywhere with him. Normally, in my arms, between my legs, he's like someone possessed, like a child, like a dervish ecstatic over the scrap of food he's been given.

This Monique is powerful. In barely an hour in my home without me, she managed to conquer everyone.

Slimane, my eldest son, was also bewitched by her. The girls told me how happy he was around Monique. He spoke to her in French. In French. He was proud. Proud of what, exactly? Monique congratulated him. Bravo! Bravo, Slimane! He looked at her with loving eyes, apparently.

I'll deal with Slimane later, undo the spell she cast over him, too.

I WOKE KHADIJA IN the middle of the night. We went into the garden of the National Library. It was very dark and a bit chilly.

I took Khadija's hands in mine.

I spoke with Khadija.

I opened Khadija's eyes.

I told her about the glorious future I have in mind for her. An important man from the Royal Palace, from the ministries, who will notice her beauty, pay tribute to her beauty, treat her like a queen. A man that I'll choose myself, for her.

I'll show you how to seduce him, my Khadija, how to make him do whatever you want. Your studies aren't working out for you, I know. It's no big deal. There are other paths in life. You are beautiful. I am your mother. Don't be naive. Don't be too innocent. You weren't meant to be a maid. As long as I live, that will never happen. We're here now, in Rabat, we have arrived in Rabat. Only a wall separates us from the palace where the king lives. Do you understand, my little girl, my sweetheart? And that wall, we will break it, we will destroy it. We will choose a rich man from the Royal Palace and make him do what we want. Listen to me, my daughter. This is what we'll do. We must be cunning with that Monique, who has already eaten your father's brain and heart. She made him blind, stupid, small. Don't be afraid, I'm here. I want to protect you. You're only fifteen years old. But this isn't the time to be weak. Don't be ashamed. There's no shame in thinking about your future and how to succeed in life. No matter the means. You're so beautiful, Khadija. It's been barely a year since we came here, to Rabat, and each day I see just how much attention you get from the important men who come to this library, the men who walk in the streets of this rich neighborhood. They want you. They devour you with their eyes. They fall for you. But they won't make the first move. They don't dare. Men never make the first move. I'll show you what to do when we find the right one, the man who'll help make your dreams come true. Our dreams. You'll marry him and we'll all be saved, rescued from want. Do you understand, Khadija? Are you with me, Khadija? Do you love me, my little girl? Tell me that you love me.

I love you, of course, my mother.

Your father is a man like all the rest. Just a man. He knows nothing. He does nothing. He's kind. Nothing more. And I have no other choice than to be stronger than him all while playing the role of the poor woman. He doesn't have any foresight. He only thinks about Wednesday nights and Saturday nights, when I let him be with me, enter me. Do you understand? Sex. Your father thinks of nothing else. He's dominated by it. That's the be all and end all for him. I'm the one who convinced him that he had to leave the bled, Béni Mellal, to flee his brother El-Bouhali who despised him, flee his sister Messaouda who controlled him. I'm the one who did everything so that we would end up here, in this library, this city, the capital. Right by Hassan II. Your father said that he was attached to his land, that he would never leave his land. I'm a Mellali from Béni Mellal: he always said. He's too sentimental, too soft, too small-minded. I'm the one, Khadija, who does everything. I'm the one who saved him from his sister Messaouda, the whore who had him wrapped around her finger. She married him off and made him divorce whenever she wanted. There's something strange going on between them. It's bizarre. It's as if they weren't brother and sister. Messaouda came to see me in the mausoleum of Saint Moulay Brahim where life had spat me up. Everyone had turned their backs on me after my first husband died in Indochina. I was living there, sleeping there, in that mausoleum. I was helping visitors to perform the rites. They gave me a bit of money. Just enough to survive. I was desperate. I had done everything I could for Allal. My duty as a spouse, as a widow. I mourned him for months. An entire year. And then I understood that I had to open my eyes once again. Pick myself up. All alone. Change. Yes, my little Khadija, there was no other choice. I had become less than nothing. Almost a beggar. Even my own father acted as if I didn't exist anymore.

His second wife had completely denatured him, transformed him into someone I didn't recognize anymore when I happened to pass him in the bled. I would hide and watch him from a distance. My father who was no longer my father. I had to wake up, Khadija. I had to cross a line that I had never really noticed before. Stop thinking that I was someone good, that my heart was pure and the sky was really blue. The sky is not blue, Khadija. It's just an illusion. A distortion. We don't know how to see. Mankind has a talent for one thing: inventing lies and living inside of them, convincing ourselves that it's the truth. My first husband, Allal, had his secret tomb. I completed this strange and necessary mission: bury an invisible body. And my eyes had gone dry, dry. Die? Keep on living? To my great surprise, I wanted to stay in this life. So I had to enter into a new skin, Khadija. Change. Change my heart. Tear out my former heart and replace it with another. And eat the world. Devour the world. Kill the world. That's the only thing that works, evidently.

Do you remember Messaouda, my little Khadija?

A bit. Vaguely. The last time I saw her, we were still in the bled, in Béni Mellal.

Messaouda came to see me in the Sidi Moulay Brahim mausoleum where I had taken refuge. She proposed that I marry her brother, Mohammed. Your father, Mohammed. She said that he was a good man, a gentle man. A timid man who didn't know how to act around women. And that was why she was the one in charge of finding him wives. She said that she had married him off several times to friends of hers but that those women had always ended up growing tired of him and asking for a divorce. He's been hurt by women, Malika. He needs a real woman, like you, Malika.

Messaouda was one of the prostitutes who used to visit the Sidi Moulay Brahim mausoleum regularly. Both to receive the blessing and also to find clients. I never liked Messaouda and I still don't. But I'll admit to you, Khadija, that I respected her. She was honest. She didn't try to make herself seem like someone she wasn't. Yes, I'm Messaouda, I open my legs for men and they pay me, very well. Yes, I'm a villain and a sorceress. Yes, you should be wary of me, stay away from me. Yes, I have a brother, Mohammed, who doesn't know how to be alone in this world without me, without me telling him where to walk, where to sit, where to sleep, and even how to breathe. Mohammed is a man who isn't like other men. He won't give you any real trouble, Malika. He needs a woman to keep him in line. I know that you'll be that woman to a tee.

I appreciated Messaouda's candidness. I found it courageous, even noble. She was a prostitute and had absolutely no shame. She was a prostitute and she was helping her brother. She was a prostitute and older than me. She had seen hard, cruel, dirty things in this merciless world. She knew better than me. She didn't wear any mask with me, that day.

I didn't have to think it over much. It was an opportunity I couldn't miss. I accepted the deal she offered me immediately.

She gave me a long hug. And she continued to lay out the conditions of this marriage. I give my brother to you, Malika. But on the condition that you always let me come to your home. Whenever I want. Whenever I need to take a break from prostitution and its exhausting nights. You will always welcome me into your home, and respectfully. You won't insult me and you'll also let me be affectionate with the children you have with my brother. Do we have a deal, Malika? I know your story, Malika. What life did to you after Allal's death in Indochina. From a distance, I've followed all the twists and turns. I know that soon you'll become a beggar, you've reached rock bottom. Alone in the world. Even Merzougue has gone. Even he ended up sorting himself out. He got married, Merzougue. That made me laugh. Merzougue married to a woman . . . Everything is possible in life. Even he ended up finding a place to live in this bled. Malika, look at me. I'm being frank. I'm putting it all on the table. Every condition. I'll save you, give you a man, a husband. My brother. You'll be respectable again, thanks to me. You'll have a family. The world will leave you alone. You won't end up a prostitute like me. Do you understand? In exchange for all this, you'll give me a place among you. Always. A place alongside you. You won't forget? Do we have a deal? A place for my old age, when men have had enough of me and my ruined body. A place where I can die. I don't want to die alone. Old and alone. I'm already forty. And one other thing, very important: you won't turn my brother against me, you won't change him. You won't stop me from seeing your children, from loving them and even taking a part in their education in my own way. And you'll grant me the honor of choosing the name of your first child. What do you say to all this, Malika?

I bowed my head to show that I was in total agreement. Her conditions seemed reasonable to me at the time.

I surmised correctly that Messaouda's power was much greater than she let on. I could already perceive her dangerous nature, the bad part, the diabolical side. But how could I judge her? It was impossible, she was what she was. And she didn't put on the airs of a respectable woman in front of me. I don't know whether or not I liked Messaouda, but I respected her. Yes. And I followed her proposal to the letter. It was an opportunity, Khadija.

I let Messaouda choose the first name of my first son. Slimane.

And I welcomed her as often as she wanted into our home.

And then, one day, I saw that I had to flee, put miles and miles of distance between me and her. When she learned about my plan from Mohammed, she came to see me and showed me another face. The face of evil. She threatened me: I'll follow you, Malika. I curse you. My ancestors and I, we curse you. I know the best sorcerers in this bled. They'll give me the most evil spells that I will then unleash on you. You won't get far, Malika. I'll find you again. And I'll have my revenge. The woman who will defeat me has not yet been born. Do you hear me, Malika, you ingrate? You hear me, Malika, whom I saved from ruin? You won't steal my brother Mohammed from me so easily. My brother was mine long before he was yours. Mohammed was my man before he was your man. I know Mohammed's secrets much better than you. You will not take him from me.

Messaouda's work didn't bother me. I knew that she was sleeping with French men, cops, soldiers, and the French farmers of Béni Mellal. I said nothing. I let her bring us food, give all you children presents, including you, Khadija, with money earned from prostitution. I didn't intervene. I respected the pact. But it was her power over Mohammed that ended up becoming intolerable to me and pushed me to defy her.

Mohammed wasn't only married to me. At the end of the day, Messaouda was his real wife. She was the one he listened to and she was the one he defended all too often. And only God knows what went on between them when I wasn't there. Everything in Mohammed's mind and body obeyed Messaouda, was shaped according to Messaouda's desires. I believe she cast spells on him. I'm certain of it. Mohammed trembled before her. He bowed his head and nearly kissed his sister's feet. I caught them countless times in a strange kind of intimacy, a couple's intimacy, in the middle of discussing, murmuring things in each other's ears using crude words, dirty words, shameful words, sexual words. I was shocked. I was not Mohammed's wife—she was.

I tolerated all of this for more than ten years. Messaouda as the first wife of her own brother. And then, one day, I went on the offensive. I came up with a plan. I did everything to convince him that we had to leave, flee, emigrate to the city. The future was the city now. And I too cast a spell on Mohammed. It worked.

We left on a long journey. The whole family wandering and in extreme poverty. From douar to douar. City to city. I'll tell you about that another time, that past, that hell. The emigration within the country. How we arrived in Rabat, the capital. How we managed to find a chaouche position for your father at the National Library that shares a wall with the Royal Palace.

Mohammed, your father, I saved him, from the bled and from his sister Messaouda. Now, we must save him from Monique. Keep that Monique out of our lives. Stop her from destroying everything we've worked so hard to build over all these years. We are close to our goal. So close. I won't let anyone stop our progress, impose other paths on us, divide us. And you, my beautiful Khadija, you will help me. You won't be a maid in Monique's home. Do you hear me? As long as I'm alive, never. *Never.*

Those of higher social standing see us as poor people, only as poor people. Not as human beings capable of reflection, of raising ourselves up, of cherishing dreams for ourselves that are big and robust. They want to help us, they say. They want to help us by pushing us down, by deciding what our place is in life. Small roles for small people. And then they say that we have no ambition, that we're too submissive before Allah. Before mektoub. Before destiny. They mock us, Khadija, us together with our beliefs, our mausoleums, our saints. For them, it's folklore. Our very lives are folklore. I've seen them and heard them laughing at us in the halls of the National Library. They see us as savages. You, Khadija, so beautiful and pure, they see you that way, too. You are nothing to them. Nothing. But I, I won't let them take away your beauty. Lock up your beauty. Use your beauty as decoration, an embellishment. You won't be Monique's slave. You hear me? Deep down, I have nothing against Monique. She acts as they all act here, the rich and the French, as if colonization weren't over. I'm not mad at Monique. But she's the one who started the war. What does she expect? That I'll roll over and let her enter my home in my absence, that I'll allow her to choose a little maid from among my daughters? No. No. I am your mother. I am the one who brought you into this world, who raised you, fed you. I am the one who nursed you when you fell ill. Don't be afraid of me, my little Khadija. I might be mean, harsh, pig-headed, stone-headed, as Mohammed says each day. Life made me this way. Survival doesn't make us into better people. And it's too late to turn back now. I won't change and I don't want to change. I don't even know what Monique looks like. I feel as if I'm waging war against a phantom. A powerful spirit. You see what I mean, Khadija? Monique is only the name of that powerful spirit. Monique is not, deep down, our enemy. She is just an envelope containing something else. We have to keep away from that danger, burn that envelope. That's our mission. Here's what you'll do.

You'll go work in Monique's villa, in the Orangers neighborhood. It's not far from the National Library. But only for two weeks. During those two weeks, you'll have access to Monique's private life, to the innermost reaches of her routine, her furniture, her clothing. Her kitchen and her bathroom. Her terrace and her garden. You'll be there day and night. You'll observe everything very attentively. You'll record it all in your head and, at the end of the first week, you'll come back and tell me every detail about Monique's life, and that of her husband and their two sons. I want to know everything, everything about them. Everything about her. I want you to strip her bare in front of me. Her faults, her fixations, her filth. I want you to enter her existence without her permission. As she did, without consulting me, without my blessing, how she entered my home, ate in my home and, with her beautiful white skin, seduced everyone in the family. You'll do this, Khadija. I'm not giving you a choice. And when you go back for the second week, I'll give you three spells. The first you'll put under Monique's bed, the second you'll cast on her clothes, and the third in her shoes. To each his methods, his weapons. Sorcery is only the first step, a way for us to protect ourselves from the evil, even if unconscious, of others, a way to leave our malevolent trace where people live without a care in the world, people who supposedly want what's best for us, who want to love us and help us. Sorcery is a science, my little Khadija. Our science to change the cruel and unjust world. Our science to keep the powerful from doing what they want. We resist with our sorcery. And they want to laugh at us, mock us, transform us into ridiculous folklore, say that none of it exists, let them say it. Sorcery exists. Our vision of the world exists. It's them who know nothing. Don't even try to convince them that this art surpasses the boundaries of the world, of the earth and sky. That it's here, deep within the earth, deep within our hearts. Here, visible and invisible. I beg you, my little Khadija, don't listen to them when they speak in front of you about our sorcery as something practiced by illiterates. Let them express their arrogance and their self-importance. All they do is show just how narrow-minded they are, just how small their own world is. Don't stop them. And, deep within you, laugh, laugh hard at them. They don't know. They don't see. That's all.

In Monique's villa, you will enact my revenge for me. And if, by chance, the spells don't produce a satisfactory result and this Monique doesn't give up, then I will move to the second stage. I will transform her life into hell and I will sow disorder into her relationship and hatred into her family. I can do it,

Khadija. At the mausoleum of Saint Moulay Brahim, they taught me things. I know the secrets of evil. And I know how to apply them, without hesitation. I know how to be completely heartless.

But we're not there yet. First things first. Conquer Monique's villa. Learn all about her cleanliness and her filth.

Perhaps I'm asking too much of you, Khadija. Forgive me. I am your mother. I must defend you to the end. I don't know any other way. One day, you'll thank me. It's not me who wants to sell you, it's your father. It's not me who doesn't see the purity in your heart. It's Monique.

You are a queen, Khadija. I'll say it again and again. You deserve a pathway lined with gold and diamonds. Not a kitchen in a bourgeois home where you'll spend your life doing dishes. Your hands, your eyes, and your sex were made for another destiny. Come give me a hug, tell me that you understand everything and that you'll carry out this plan.

The night in the National Library's garden is on our side. The night is our witness. Our pillar. Even the moon, look, look, there she is, full, beautiful, to give us her blessing.

Come here. Come, Khadija. Don't cry. No one deserves your tears yet. The door has not yet completely closed on us. I am here. We are alive. Alive. There's still a chance to escape poverty as our destiny, as an inevitability. You're only fifteen years old, my girl.

THE FIRST WEEK, MONIQUE was wonderful to Khadija. She wasn't a temperamental boss, or a bourgeois woman who moralizes all the time.

She showed Khadija everything in the villa, every room. She opened every cabinet in front of her. And in the kitchen, she said: I'll show you how to prepare French meals, and maybe you'll be able to make them for your own family. She said all this not with French words but with Arabic words, Moroccan words.

She's just arrived in Morocco and already she's joined us in our own language. When did she have time to learn it?

Khadija reminded me that Monique was born here, in Casablanca. She lived here until she was ten years old. Her nanny, a woman named Batoule, spoke to her in Moroccan Arabic. And, evidently, she hasn't forgotten it.

It's strange. Khadija says that Monique seems sincere.

Her Arabic isn't perfect, but she makes an effort. She smiles. She's sincere, my mother.

With a few Moroccan Arabic words, Monique has managed to seduce Khadija right off the bat. She's much more dangerous than I thought. What is the source of her power? Being French? Being a bourgeois French woman?

Khadija says that, from up close, she is beyond beautiful, really very, very beautiful. Even in the morning, even without makeup, she's beautiful. With nothing at all, she's beautiful.

Khadija daydreams and says: I would so love to be like her.

Think of your future, my Khadija. Let me remind you that I agreed to send you to her villa for one specific reason, and not for you to fall in love with her. Wake up, Khadija. Don't be like your father. Too naive, too limited in your power, too limited in your way of judging people and the world. Wake up. This Monique already has everything she wants in life. She is free to adopt whatever persona she chooses. Kind and generous with you today, haughty and disdainful tomorrow, after you've fallen entirely into her trap. She lives in a villa. We are nine people who live in two small rooms.

Khadija tells me that Monique has already given her two gifts.

I answer viciously:

At Monique's house, where do you eat? In the kitchen, right? Not with her around the same table as her and her family. You eat all alone in the kitchen. Like a dog thrown the scraps from others' plates. You're not a dog, Khadija. And I forbid you from making French dishes in my home that she teaches you in her villa. Understand?

Khadija is so young. I see it clearly now. I don't have a choice. I must continue to make decisions for her. Continue to be vicious with her.

Listen up, Khadija. You have a week left working in Monique's house. A week to carry out our plans. I've prepared the spells that you'll cast in her house, under her bed, on her furniture, on her clothing. And I even have a spell for you to cast on her food. I am your mother. And you will obey my orders. Stop daydreaming about the garden of her villa. You've never seen anything so beautiful, you say. Well, that's because you're only fifteen, Khadija. You haven't seen anything in life yet. You too will have a villa and a large garden in the Orangers neighborhood. Nothing is impossible.

Khadija, here are the spells. You will do as I say. I don't want to hear any more out of you. It's as though she's the one in charge of you now, not me.

Khadija tried to defend Monique once more.

I slapped her.

I shouldn't have slapped Khadija. It was a clear sign of Monique's resounding victory, the very proof of my defeat.

Khadija didn't cry.

The next morning, I woke her up early and gave her the four spells to cast in Monique's home. I could tell from her eyes that she hadn't really slept, that she had been thinking during the night and had come to understand that I was right.

I made Khadija food. Mint tea. Bread. Olive oil. I squeezed her in my arms. And I sent her to Monique's house.

I watched her from the door of the National Library. She went down the little hill toward the Orangers neighborhood.

She disappeared between the white villas. At no point did she turn around to wave at me. To reassure me. To tell me that she loves me more than she loves Monique.

I understood then that it was useless. Khadija is like her father. Weak. Soft. Too soft. Unreliable.

At the end of this second week, Khadija will return and tell me that she didn't cast the spells in the villa. Who knows what she'll come up with to justify this betrayal.

I'll have to do it on my own. Accomplish my mission through different means. Find another way to resist the invasion of Monique and her world.

MOROCCO NEVER OBTAINED INDEPENDENCE in 1956. They've been lying to us. The king, his ministers, and the rich tricked us. They're making a mockery of us. They anesthetize us a little more each day as they continue to fulfill their own plans. To divide up the riches among themselves.

France is still here.

Monique's husband came to Morocco with a very specific mission: choose young men in good health to send to France. To build France. Rebuild France.

We are nothing at all. Just cattle. They can choose whoever they want, choose our place and our destiny. Decide what our lives will be, and our deaths.

We are not people like them. They know better. We are simpletons. Of course. Simpletons deserve to be slaves. We're born into it.

Here, in Morocco, and over there, in France, it's the same exploitation.

Monique can say what she wants, be so kind, so generous, so sweet, have the purest heart there ever was, but she takes part in this exploitation in her own way.

I HAVE NOTHING AGAINST you, Monique. But I need to get you out of my life.

I lost my husband Allal. I won't lose my daughter Khadija.

I know for sure now that Khadija has been bewitched by you, it's as though she's in love with you. She not only dared to disobey me but, on top of it, she had the nerve to tell me a story about Monique in an attempt to make me change my mind about her.

A beautiful story, she told me. Listen, Maman, listen before you judge her.

My father, Mohammed, came to see me last Wednesday afternoon, in Monique's villa. To see how it was going, my job in her home. He rang the bell. I opened the villa door. And we spoke, outside, for about ten minutes. Then Monique joined us and insisted that Mohammed enter the villa. She brought us to the garden. She invited us to sit down around the table. And she said: It's four o'clock. Time for a snack, don't you think? Moroccan-style steamed milk with a little coffee in it, how does that sound? With Moroccan donuts, *chfanj*, does that sound good? We said yes. Monique asked me to go buy a kilo at the *chafnaje*, which isn't far from the villa. She pronounced those Moroccan words perfectly: "chfanj" and "chafnaje." That made me smile. When I returned, Monique had finished preparing the milk with coffee. A lot of milk and not too much coffee, the way you do it, Maman. I placed the kilo of chfanj on a lovely big white plate. And we went back to the garden, where Mohammed was waiting. We drank all the milk with coffee and ate all the donuts. Monique ate as much as we did. Without any fuss. She ate the donuts with her hands, Maman. And the oil from the donuts dripped between her fingers and even down her chin. Like us, me and Mohammed. That made us laugh. A lot. It was a beautiful moment, Maman. Very beautiful. We were happy, simply happy to be there, the three of us. Monique was the happiest, I think. Monique is not a fake woman. That's not her style. You see? You see, Maman? She welcomed Mohammed very nicely. She gave us her time. It was sincere. At no point did we feel a form of superiority or snobbery on her part. Mohammed was delighted. He saw with his own eyes how I was treated by Monique, in Monique's villa. And that really reassured him, I think. Did he tell you about his visit to Monique's house, Maman?

Before letting him leave, Monique gave Mohammed a present. She said: You're the same size as my husband, Alain. I have something for you. A suit he doesn't wear anymore. A suit from Paris. Both of you, come with me upstairs.

We followed her to her bedroom. She opened the closet and took out a magnificent light blue suit. Mohammed went into the bathroom to try it on. When he came back out, Monique cried: Oooh la la la! Mohammed was a new person, Maman. Truly. The color and fit of the suit transformed him into a real dandy, a city slicker. Monsieur Mohammed. Ssi Mohammed. Not a poor country bumpkin, a meskine from Béni Mellal, anymore. He was so, so pleased, it was obvious. He couldn't stop smiling. He felt honored, I think. And we, Monique and I, sized him up happily. We smiled and said: Ooohhh la la la, Mohammed! And he answered: Ooohhh la la la! Oooohhhh la la la laaaaa! It lasted for at least fifteen minutes, that moment.

Monique also gave him one of Alain's old white shirts.

My father looked very handsome. It was funny. He kept clowning around. I'll never forget the look on his face. His face, Maman. He looked like an important—and slightly ridiculous—man. He even dared to approach Monique and, like a French man, give her a distinguished kiss on the hand. Monique let him. She played along. She even did one better: she took my father's hands and invited him to dance. Can you imagine, Maman? They danced, danced before me, Maman. Mohammed and Monique.

Monique and Mohammed. They danced. Mohammed rose to the occasion. I was not at all ashamed of him.

And while they danced, Monique started to sing. A very beautiful French song. She told me the name: "Bambino." And the name of the singer, Dalida. She told me that Dalida is Egyptian. An Egyptian from Egypt who sings in French, who has an Arab name, Dalida, and who is famous in France with her Arab name.

Monique said: Bambino, bambino. And we, Mohammed and I, repeated after her: Bambino, bambino. Again. Again. And again.

I know a French song now. Bambino, bambino. It's easy. Bambino, bambino. Dalida. Dalida. Bambino, bambino.

Monique is generous. Delightful. You see, Maman? You see?

Did Mohammed show you the light blue suit, Maman?

MONIQUE, WE DON'T NEED your charity.

I will enter your night, Monique, your dreams, and overthrow you. I will go to the Jewish quarter of the Rabat medina, to the most powerful sorcerer, Moussa, and he'll help me bring you down. If need be, I'll sell my only treasure: my gold bracelet. I'm prepared to do it, to impoverish myself even more.

Very soon, I'll find the right husband for Khadija, an important man. Moussa will help with that too, to catch that man, make him fall for her.

Giving you Khadija, Monique, would mean accepting my fate without saying or doing a thing about it. It would mean killing Allal a second time.

I want money, too. I want to sail through life from above. Through Khadija, I want to attract good fortune and share it with my other children. That's my right. That's my goal. That's my war.

Monique, you can stay in Morocco as long as you want. That's not up to me. You can leave, come back, leave again and come back again. I don't care. But far from me. Far from us. Far from my daughter. I ask nothing else.

With my two hands, I will pry open Khadija's heart and remove all the traces you're trying to leave there.

Monique, I know about your father. Khadija told me everything.

You have a grave in Rabat.

Your father died here when you were nine. And a year later, the whole family returned to France, to Paris.

You told Khadija that you never got used to France. You didn't know what you were doing there. You didn't understand the people there. You weren't like them, French like them.

I'M NOT FRENCH. I was born here, in Casablanca. I am from here. I am Moroccan, too. And for more than twenty years now, I've wanted only one thing, dreamt of only one thing: to return. To live in Morocco.

Live in your light.

Live alongside my father, Georges, whom I hadn't visited in so many years. He misses me. My father appears at night in my sleep, in my dreams. He stands there, in my dreams. He stares at me. He reproaches me. He is so alone in his grave.

I did everything to urge my husband, Alain, to accept the job he was offered here: find Moroccan workers to send to France. He didn't want to, at first. He didn't understand. The more I spoke of my father, the more I saw in his eyes that he thought I was crazy. You're losing your mind, Monique. Come back to your senses, Monique. I had to threaten him before he gave in. For me, it was now or never. I had to answer my father's call. I don't see what's so crazy about that. Honoring the dead and nurturing them is the most natural thing in the world, isn't it? Otherwise, what use are the living? Just to live for themselves?

I abandoned my father a long time ago. I am ashamed. I am ashamed.

We are here now. I am here. I have returned. To Morocco. To Rabat. My father and his grave are nearby. In the Christian cemetery, not far from the cliffs that look directly over the Atlantic Ocean.

I can finally breathe. Repair a void in me that was bigger than I imagined. Walk through my memories as a young girl. Rediscover them, relive them, make them real. Make the past into a present. And who cares what people might say, how they might criticize me. This is a very personal matter. I am compelled by a desire that's bigger than me. Something that I understand very well and that, at the same time, I have no wish to normalize completely.

My father doesn't want to stay here alone. He needs us. Me most of all.

Georges. I didn't call him "Papa." He wanted me to call him by his first name. That shocked Maman, Yvette, at first. And later, it amused her. She called us "the couple." Georges and Monique. When is the wedding of Monique and Georges? She laughed at us. And that made me furious. I was five, six years old at the time. Papa is mine. Papa is mine.

When it was nice out, Georges sometimes brought me, on Sundays, to walk along the banks of the Bou Regreg River.

We're walking on the Rabat side. Georges says: On the other side of the river, there's another world, Monique. It's called Salé. It's an ancient city, more ancient than Rabat. Over there, the people are crazy. Crazy and kind. Shall we go say hello to them, Monique?

Yes, yes, Georges. Let's go see the crazy people.

Each time, we take the same small boat to cross the Bou

Regreg River. Georges says: Here, this boat is called *flouka*. Say it. *Flouka*. The flouka belongs to Jelloul. A man with a very nice mustache, like Georges.

We are in the flouka. It's only us: the mustached men, Georges and Jelloul, and me. I watch them. My men. I'm happy. We're walking on water. Georges speaks with Jelloul in Moroccan Arabic. Jelloul is gentle, timid. A man of few words. He smiles.

Jelloul. It's incredible how well I still remember Jelloul and his little smiles. His eyes watching me. The funny faces he makes at me. I laugh. Georges doesn't intervene. He lets us have these small moments that mean nothing at all but that, from then on, are absolutely everything for me.

Jelloul. Where are you now? Are you still alive?

We arrive on the other side, on the other shore. In the other world. In Salé. Georges says that even the air in Salé is not the same air as in Rabat, even though the cities are just opposite each other, separated by this river. You'll see, Monique. The people here don't act like the people in Rabat. They're rivals. You'll see. There's something peculiar.

I'm seven. I don't understand. But I believe Georges. We're in Salé. We're walking to Salé. We're heading for the city of Salé.

Georges says again: We're going to where the Arabs live. Don't be afraid, Monique. They're just Arabs. They're very kind. I don't know why Georges says that. I know that Jelloul is very, very kind. Loyal and kind. He waits for us on the bank of the river to bring us back to Rabat later. He won't take other passengers. He waits for us. Just us. Jelloul couldn't be mean. It's impossible. Jelloul is all of Morocco.

In Salé, we walk for a long time down the side streets, in the souk, in the public squares. We'll get lost here, Monique. Let's get lost in Salé, Georges. The Arabs sometimes stare at us adamantly. Some men stop us and gently touch my head, my hair.

They smile. They leave. Georges always let them do it. Touch me. Caress me. Make my acquaintance in this way. If I concentrate, I think I could conjure all the faces of those men of Salé who touched my head. I could do it. I will do it.

We do nothing else in Salé. We walk. We walk. And, at a certain point, we enter an Arab café, in the middle of a square where people are selling old things. We sit there, among them: the Arabs. We look at them. It doesn't bother them, I think. It's like a spectacle, their life, a game, theater. Our presence doesn't bother them, I'm sure of it. They live their lives without really paying attention to us.

That Arab café in Salé, I'll find it again easily.

Georges is still there. He's waiting for me. Jelloul is with him. They are as before. Mustached as before. They drink mint tea, side by side. They're very close to each other. They tell each other things, in Moroccan Arabic. They even touch. Georges places his hand on Jelloul's hand. Jelloul doesn't pull away. They stare at each other. They smile at each other. They love each other. There is something between them that I didn't understand when I was seven. That I see perfectly, clearly, now. That I understand perfectly, clearly, now. The romantic and sexual bond between my father and Morocco, between Georges and Jelloul. Between men.

I'm on the way back. I'm tired. Georges takes me in his arms. We walk. We walk. The sun is about to set.

Georges and I, we can't wait, can't wait, can't wait to see Jelloul again. Will Jelloul be there? Did Jelloul wait for us, as promised?

We walk. We walk. We approach the Bou Regreg River. We see Rabat on the other side. Georges and I, we think of only one thing: Jelloul.

We are both in love with Jelloul.

Jelloul. Jelloul. Jelloul.

I came back to Morocco.

I will never leave again.

KHADIJA WAS VERY TOUCHED by your story, Monique. She was crying when she recounted your words to me. And I, I was shocked, devastated.

I see a new wall standing before me: Monique's Moroccan past. Monique's Moroccan legitimacy. I can't take it away from her, I can't fight against it, and I don't want to let these complications that don't concern me into my head. It's not my history. It's not my past.

Although sincere and shaken up, Monique wants only one thing: to occupy all the space. Monique Monique Monique. Everywhere. Everywhere. She is the star, the little girl who misses her father dearly. She is the most important. And we, we are apparently only details, confidants, servants ready to listen to her, help her, soothe her, understand her, be there for her always.

She probably doesn't realize to what extent her behavior excludes us and belittles us. To what extent she holds power over us. She appears, and everyone is dumbstruck by her beauty, her refinement, and by her skin, so white. She speaks, and everyone immediately forgets who they are. The world instantly begins to revolve around Monique: Monique's desires. Monique's past. Monique's suffering. Monique's sublime fragility. Monique is the heroine of a film, of a play. Or who knows what else.

Monique is a dangerous woman.

Hypnotized, we all trail behind her. Even me, Malika.

In Monique's villa, Khadija feels as though she's at the very center of a rich and romantic life. For her, Monique is an opportunity, someone to follow no matter what, to imitate in every way. I am only a country bumpkin who goes to the hammam just once per month. Nothing more. I don't wear perfume. I don't wear makeup. I wear a caftan and a djellaba, not skirts and blouses.

Khadija has forgotten what I taught her. She has forgotten my words. The promise we made that night in the garden of the National Library.

She didn't even try to cast the spells that I gave her in Monique's villa.

Instead, she spoke to me of Monique's father as if he were her own father.

In so little time, my daughter has stopped being my daughter.

Monique brought her to the Christian cemetery of Rabat. They looked for her father's grave. It took them a long time. And when they finally found it, Monique immediately lay down on the grave.

She was not afraid. She embraced the grave. She closed her eyes. It was strange, Maman. Very strange. And, at the same time, it was beautiful. Monique and her father, reuniting. I cried, Maman.

Monique asked my daughter to find the cemetery caretaker. And the three of them ripped out the weeds surrounding the grave.

Monique participated. With her own hands. Like us, Maman. And, when it was done, she gave a lot of money to the caretaker. Five dirhams. That's a lot, Maman.

Monique is kind. She's very kind. Really, Maman. I could never do her harm, cast spells in her villa. I'm sorry. I have seen only good in her, Maman. I'm sorry. Don't be cruel to her. You have to give her a chance. She's not like you say. Not at all, I swear, Maman. She doesn't treat me like a maid. Give her a chance.

You're jealous of Monique, Maman.

If only it was a simple matter of jealousy. Khadija knows nothing about me, her own mother. Nothing of my past, my history, my suffering, my poverty, my parents in the bled who threw me in the streets after Allal. Nothing. And, in two weeks, she knows everything about this Monique. She even cleared her father's grave. She comforted her. And I, her own mother, I get none of that from her, none of that curiosity for my past. None of that empathy. None of that understanding.

What did I do in life to deserve this, the ingratitude of my own daughter?

Maybe I am jealous of Monique. Of course I'm jealous of Monique.

And yet I've never seen Monique. I don't know Monique. Does Monique really exist? Does Monique think of me as I think of her? No. Of course not.

I have no choice but to take the next step. Enact my vengeance on my own.

I TOLD HER TO meet me in Chellah, just outside of Rabat, on the other side of the tall rampart that surrounds the entire city.

The path to the Chellah ruins was deserted. The sun was already beating down intensely. It was two in the afternoon. Almost everyone was napping.

It would take me more than an hour to arrive at the meeting place.

I put on my green djellaba. I covered a part of my face with my black veil.

I left the National Library. And I started to walk.

I crossed Bab Rouah. The Gate of the Winds. To the left, the path leads toward the center of town. That's not my path. I have to go straight, then turn left, passing in front of the Moulay Youssef High School. Yes. From there, continue straight ahead. At the end of this road lie the Chellah ruins.

I said nothing to Mohammed, nor to my other children.

Only Khadija knows. Tell Monique that I'll wait for her next to the pond of sacred eels in Chellah. Tell her that, if she happens to arrive before me, she must not go to the pond without me. I am the one who must bring her there. Make sure you stress this point. Tell her also that I'll be wearing a green djellaba. And even though I've never seen her before, there's no need to worry: I'll be able to recognize her.

I know her, Monique, without knowing her.

I can even smell her scent already, so much have people spoken to me about her and her body.

On the path to Chellah, I see her without seeing her, I follow her and I precede her. I am her shadow. She isn't wary of me. She is mistaken.

The pond of sacred eels of Chellah. I'll be sitting on the steps, protected by the coolness of the foliage that surrounds it and reinforces its magic, its baraka. I will be there first and I will have plenty of time to think about how to accomplish my plan. Rid myself of Monique for good. Aided, supported by the spirits of Chellah, by the graves and tombs of Chellah, by the ancestors who, long before the French arrived in Morocco, hid in Chellah the mythical treasures waiting to be discovered. Last night, I summoned them, I called them, our ancestors. They will be on my side, surely on my side, against Monique.

Salomon and his ring are in Chellah. I was told that as soon as we arrived in Rabat. And the golden eel of Chellah really exists. Perhaps, if I'm lucky, it will emerge from its hole at the very bottom of the spring and it will speak to me.

Chellah is my territory. These are our spirits. These are our former combatants of previous centuries. These are our vestiges I'm walking on. This path runs along the ramparts of Rabat. Monique knows nothing about all this. I imagine that Chellah is nothing for her but a place of the past, ruins of the past, something romantic. It's pretty, it's beautiful, it's magnificent, she'll say.

Bab Rouah is behind me. I walk straight ahead. Then I'll turn right, by the Moulay Youssef High School.

I pass by an enormous gate. There are police officers, soldiers, guards. All Black. I stop. I don't understand. What is this gate? I look at what lies behind it. Another path, very long, very well maintained, at the end of which is another gate, just as enormous. In the middle of this path, an esplanade and, to the right, a grandiose gate, green and gold. I'm far away but I see it, this gate, very clearly.

Is it the Royal Palace?

Yes. Of course. The Royal Palace. And all that surrounds it is the Touarga neighborhood. Where the Black slaves and servants of the king live.

It's the official entrance to Hassan II's palace.

Where I live, in the National Library's garden, there is only one wall between us and the Palace. A very high wall. Often, my children stick their ears against this wall to listen to what's happening on the other side. They love to spy on the king. During summer vacation, since they have nothing else to do, they stay glued to the wall for hours and hours, daydreaming, fantasizing, hallucinating. And sometimes they say: It's the king, it's him, I recognize his voice, he's screaming, he's angry, he's going to kill someone. And they burst into laughter.

I freeze. I have to make a decision. Should I pass by the Touarga gate and finally get a look at the Royal Palace from up close? Will they let a woman like me walk on this path, so pristine, and get a bit closer to the heart of power in this country?

I don't wait for the answer. I charge. I cross through the Touarga gate.

The guards and the soldiers, tired, crushed by the hellish sun, pay no attention to me. For them, I don't even exist. All the better.

On the other side, in Touarga, where everything in this

country is decided, where the king lives, there is a great, immense, formidable silence. The silence that follows a bomb explosion. The silence that falls when we learn of someone's violent death.

I walk in Touarga. There is no one. Absolutely no one. I imagine that they're all hidden away in the great palace but, even so, they could make a sound, give a sign of life. I don't understand. I'm walking next to the palace and no one stops me, no one notices my presence. There's no life here. Where is all the life here? Is this palace real, or is it just decor, a facade?

There is only me, alone, as though on another planet.

A woman from the bled wearing a bright green djellaba who could be spotted from a mile away.

It's very strange.

I'm not afraid. Absolutely not afraid. I look left, right, I look at the road, the cement, the sidewalks, the trees, I even look at the sky. And everything seems empty. It's there without being there. There's only me, Malika, about to take her revenge. There's only me as proof that life is still possible on this earth.

There's only me on this path.

Is King Hassan II here? Where? And his ministers?

But how can they command us, the Moroccans, from this place where there's no life?

And I, in the National Library garden, thought that important men abounded behind the wall and that Khadija, so beautiful and so regal, would have her pick!

Where are they, the important men? Where is it, their power? And their money? And how will I manage to see them here, cross paths with them here, make contact with them?

I'm in the middle of Touarga now.

I stop. I look at the incredibly large official gate of the Royal Palace. Green, gold, and blue too, from up close. Even here there's no one. No guard. No soldier. No officer. Nothing.

What is going on? Where have they all gone? To the hammam? What are they up to? Suppressing a military coup d'état that I'm not yet aware of? Is Hassan II still the king of Morocco? Is this the end?

And Medhi Ben Barka, is he there, behind that enormous gate, imprisoned, tortured, and still alive?

I think suddenly of Mehdi Ben Barka and what my first husband, Allal, told me about him.

Everyone says that he was kidnapped in France and that they never found his body. Neither alive nor dead.

Mehdi Ben Barka is not dead.

Perhaps he's here, Mehdi Ben Barka, in Touarga, just behind the enormous gate of this palace. With them. Sharing the same silence and the same absence as them. Perhaps. Where better to keep as prisoner that magnificent and revolutionary man than here, in the king's palace, with the king? No one would dare come look for him here. No one would even dare think that they would hide him here, in the palace.

Mehdi Ben Barka is here. I'm sure of it now. Here, in the home of Hassan II. Here, where Hassan II can see him whenever he likes, every day, every night. See him, torture him how he likes, when he likes. Remind him that kings always win, of course, and that the dreams of the poor never come true. Mehdi Ben Barka tried to play the role of savior. Bravo! Bravo! That worked for a time. For the son of a nearly poor family, it's honestly not bad. To become a real leader, an actual hero in the eyes of an entire people. But let's not get carried away. You don't defy the king with impunity. No one outshines the king. No one. Neither in Morocco nor anywhere else.

Should I go knock on the door of the Royal Palace and ask them to set him free?

He's a good man, you know. He's a man who cared about us, about me. He's a liberator.

He's not dead, Mehdi Ben Barka. He can't be dead. It's simply impossible. My heart tells me that he's here, in our country. Let me enter. I just want to see him. Greet him. Touch him. Have some of his baraka and his light, just a tiny bit. And, most importantly, tell him about Allal.

Don't kill Mehdi Ben Barka, please.

Let me enter.

I just want to tell him *choukran*. Thank you. From the bottom of my heart.

Ben Barka is from Rabat. I'm in Rabat. I don't fight in the same way as Ben Barka, of course. I don't have his virtue. His ambition. I don't have his vision. His generosity. I don't have his intelligence. But I'm here, in this city, on the bank of the Bou Regreg River. I walk where he walked. I live and breathe here where he was born, here where he learned to find meaning in life, his life, the life of Moroccans and all the others in the world like us.

I'm sure that Mehdi Ben Barka is still alive. He's in this palace. I'm not dreaming. I'm not delirious. Someone must free Mehdi Ben Barka. Is there anyone who can help me? Who? Who?

Go alone, Malika. You're nothing but a poor woman of this country. Everything about you exudes poverty. They wouldn't dare harm you. At worst, they'll slam the door violently in your face. Go on. Mehdi Ben Barka is here, a prisoner here, you're right. Mehdi Ben Barka is not dead.

I didn't knock on the enormous gate. I was afraid. They could kidnap me too and toss me behind the sun, in prison, once and for all. They could cut off my tongue, then my head. They could rip out my heart while I'm still alive. They can do anything.

I'm so afraid now.

The total emptiness of this royal neighborhood makes me very afraid. I look at the enormous gate. I speak.

Goodbye, Mehdi Ben Barka. I'll pray for you every night. One day, you'll be back among us. I'll speak lovingly about you to my children, just as Allal found the right words to speak to me about you before he went to Indochina.

In the dark sky, Mehdi Ben Barka will forever remain a star that shines for us.

Nothing dies. Everything is reborn.

Suddenly, the enormous gate opens wide.

A small man dressed in a white djellaba comes out. Is it Hassan II?

He walks toward me. I'm not dreaming. He looks at me. He smiles at me. He keeps walking. He stops in front of me. He says: Hello, Malika. I am Mehdi Ben Barka.

I'm not dreaming. The gate is still open behind him. And this man really is standing in front of me.

I don't know what Mehdi Ben Barka looks like.

The man stops smiling at me. He looks me straight in the eyes and he says: I am Mehdi Ben Barka. Come with me, let's sit over there, on the grass. He walks away. I watch him sit down on the grass. I think that he'll dirty his white djellaba. He signals for me to join him.

I'm next to him. He seems like a powerful Moroccan *fquih*, a judge, capable of everything, of good and evil. A fquih who has a very deep knowledge of this country. A man who keeps all the secrets and all the keys of Morocco within him. No one can really fight him anymore.

He smiles at me again. I look at his very thick eyebrows for a moment. He looks like a child now. Very sweet. I smile at him. I believe him. He is Mehdi Ben Barka. Yes, it's really you. I believe you. We are in Touarga. At the very heart of this world and at the same time apart from it.

I stop asking myself useless questions. I think of Allal. I think of the battle with Monique that lies ahead of me.

Mehdi Ben Barka prepares to speak. I get ready to receive his words as if he were the Prophet.

He takes my left hand between his two hands. What will he do? Read my life line? Reveal my future?

I withdraw my hand. I don't want to know the future.

Ben Barka understands. He doesn't insist. He says nothing. We stare at each other. For a long time.

Is that all? Mehdi Ben Barka has nothing to say to me?

I lower my eyes. I raise them again. He's still here. He hasn't disappeared. He's not smiling anymore. His eyes are closed.

Tears start to flow from Mehdi Ben Barka's eyes. Warm and uninterrupted tears. They flow. They flow. Two long rivers on his two cheeks. They flow. They flow.

There's nothing to do now. He left the palace for this. To cry in front of someone. To cry in front of me. That's all.

It lasts several minutes.

I am the witness of this truth that emerges, that explodes and has no need for words.

Just tears.

Mehdi Ben Barka's tears.

He lifts his eyes. He looks at me. I know what I must do.

With my two hands, I dry Mehdi's tears. Slowly. Softly. A mother with her son.

And then I dry my hands on my green djellaba.

There. Something has just happened. A transmission. The transmission of the spirit and the baraka—the blessing—of Mehdi Ben Barka. His battles. His failures. His sadness that endures, even here, in the afterlife. They arrested him and killed him when his dream was just beginning to unfurl, to come true. They made him disappear.

All of this is now in me. The traces of Mehdi Ben Barka's tears on my djellaba.

I'm not dreaming.

I'm so grateful. I take Ben Barka's hand in mine. I lean over to kiss him. He stops me. Very gently.

I look at him. He smiles.

And then I fall. I faint. I exit this scene. When I wake up, I'm alone, lying on the grass. Mehdi Ben Barka isn't here anymore. The enormous gate of the Royal Palace is closed as before.

I stand up.

And immediately I resume my path toward the Chellah ruins.

I feel strong. Blessed.

At the end of this path through Touarga, I will pass the second gate, and then Chellah will appear, illuminated by the summer sun. Chellah alone on the bank of the Bou Regreg River. Chellah, forgotten monument that I must arrive at first. Before Monique. Chellah: my last chance to get Monique out of my life.

MONIQUE'S SKIN IS SO white. My children were right.

I recognized her straight away.

Near the pond of the sacred eels, Monique was there, already. First. So beautiful as to seem unreal. So refined and rich it's startling. Powerful without having to do a thing except be there. Appear.

Rather than become angry at her, I felt, despite myself, strongly drawn to Monique's skin. Something in me wanted to cede to this woman immediately. I wanted to approach her, her skin, touch it and lick it. It isn't skin she has. It's milk.

White. This word has been on an endless loop in my home for two months now. My daughters, my sons, and even my husband speak and dream about Monique all the time. They sincerely adore her. They all want to be there for her, to bask in the radiance of her beauty.

I mocked them. And now that I'm standing in front of Monique, I understand. I believe I too am falling for Monique. I'm salivating and my throat is dry at the same time. I haven't even said hello to her, and already she's winning. What is happening to me?

Yes, she's beautiful, very beautiful. Yes, I've never seen such perfect, such enchanting skin in my life. Yes, she's angelic and warm. But I know what's hiding behind that mask, behind that skin.

Beauty needs men and women to appraise it and delight in it.

Monique's beauty is not for us.

This woman is a sorceress. A real sorceress. I repeat these words so as not to let her enter into my heart and change it. I look straight into Monique's eyes and I recite a short surah, a chapter from the Koran that protects from harm and the evil eye.

Monique listens to me attentively.

When I've finished my recitation, she steps toward me. She stops. I see her eyes from up close. They're blue. Incredibly blue. I am absolutely nothing faced with those eyes. Those eyes cannot exist. It's impossible. Those might be the devil's eyes. Look away, look away, Malika.

I continue to face Monique. My legs tremble.

Monique smiles. The small smile of a young, well-mannered girl. Her lips are very red. Her teeth gleam. I want to touch them, her teeth, offer them my tongue.

My God! My God! What is happening to me? Why are these ideas and temptations in my head, in my heart? My God!

I recite another surah from the Koran, one that keeps the devil away.

It's no use.

Monique takes two steps toward me. She's close, very close to me. I smell her perfume and her scent. Vetiver on white skin, in the body of a woman of utter beauty who is still walking toward me.

Milk. Vetiver. That skin. It's too much for me. I'll never be able to resist her. What does this woman want? What does she want from me?

I'm just a simple woman from Béni Mellal who's trying to find a way to ensure a beautiful future for her children. A way for us not to stay poor, destitute, for this entire life and the one after. I am no threat to Monique. And yet I am the one that destiny chose to place before her, I am the one who must be sacrificed before this woman's beauty.

But I don't want to die. I don't want to end up a slave. I don't want my children to stay small and make their way through life with their heads down, their pockets empty, with no determination, no strategy, no vision. I can't bear for people to look at us with pity and compassion. I am not a very good person. I know it. My family has told me again and again. I can be very cruel.

In Chellah, in front of Monique, it's no use. She's here. She's the queen, not me, not my daughter Khadija.

Khadija is beautiful, very beautiful. However, compared to Monique, she's nothing but a tiny star with no radiance. I have no choice but to recognize this.

I finally understand Khadija.

I must protect Khadija. Now more than ever.

Monique extends her hand to greet me.

I don't take her hand. I don't know where I find the strength for this attitude. This refusal. Monique's hand is there, suspended, near my body, near my stomach. Let her wait!

That's what she does. Monique calmly waits for me to change my mind. Then, without asking, she brings her hand to my face. She touches my black veil and, very gently, lowers it.

I'm shocked. How dare she? But, as if paralyzed, I let her do it.

Monique looks at my face.

I am bare. I'm like an exotic animal. A poor woman seen as nothing but a poor woman. A woman that someone like Monique can touch without asking for permission.

She continues to look at my face. She smiles. She smiles

kindly and honestly. She seems sincere. She feigns sincerity well. She keeps smiling.

I don't respond.

Despite myself, fascinated, I look at Monique's face. The details of Monique's face.

No makeup. On her nose and the tops of her cheeks, a few freckles, not many. I count them.

Twenty. There are twenty.

But what is happening to me in front of this French woman? I'm losing my head and losing control.

Monique has been smiling for a while now. Her smile advances toward me. It disturbs me. It perturbs me. I am utterly lost. I can't concentrate anymore. Monique can have her way with me.

Suddenly, I'm struck by the color of her hair. Orange. Like henna. There's fire in her hair. A blaze.

I don't know what comes over me. I'm no longer afraid. I too reach my hand toward Monique. I touch the blaze. Her hair is real. It was tied up in the back, Monique lets it down. I understand. It's for me. An invitation. She likes what I'm doing.

I run my fingers through Monique's hair. I take my time. Very slowly. I play. I forget myself. It's unbelievably soft.

Monique stops smiling. She closes her eyes. It seems like she's enjoying it.

I withdraw my fingers. I take a step back. I go to the right side of the pond of sacred eels.

Monique is alone. Her eyes are still closed.

The afternoon heat is unbearable.

A cool breeze suddenly reaches us. It comes and goes between me and Monique. It lifts Monique's pretty beige dress. Rustles it. It sends her hair flying in the air.

It goes in every direction. It's beautiful to see.

She clearly enjoys it. She doesn't open her eyes.

She's not a vision, this woman. She's a dream. She's beyond beauty. She's not real. There's no way I can fight against her.

The wind leaves Monique and comes to me. It's invisible, and yet I see it pursue its path toward me. It slips under my green djellaba and enters all of me. The same wind that was all around Monique is now present in me. It's soft, it's good. I don't resist. I put my transparent black veil back over my face. And I let myself be invaded by the wind. I consent. Enter all of me. Enter. And, like Monique, I close my eyes.

It's a green world, where everything is green.

Paradise?

I open my eyes.

Monique is sitting on a step of the pond of sacred eels. She's crying. Like an abandoned little girl, she cries.

I move toward her. I sit next to her. I let her cry as much as she wants. As much as she can. I won't fall into this trap.

Monique dries her tears, rearranges her hair as best she can, looks at the pond. This lasts a long time.

It's time to say what I have to say. Go on, Malika. Monique has lost her power now. Speak. Speak.

I feel some pity toward her. To see her thus, a little girl who's probably crying over her dead father, buried in Rabat, spurs tenderness in my heart for her, despite myself.

Monique has a grave in Morocco. She came back to Morocco for this grave. A grave in the Océan neighborhood, in Rabat. Her father's grave overlooks the sea.

Khadija has not stopped using this argument to defend Monique and justify her desire to stay with her in her villa in Orangers, and even to go to France with her: Monique has been blessed by life, Maman. She cannot be cruel. She is not a cruel person. She is not like the others.

Sitting next to Monique, near the pond of sacred eels, I almost agree with Khadija. I feel this woman's sincerity. Despite myself, she enters into my heart. I'm even overwhelmed by the sentiments that course through me. The little girl who cries cries cries and who, suddenly, is nothing more than that. Forever a little girl. No longer the French woman who is so beautiful, so white, who seduces everyone.

Monique needs someone to help her accomplish a ritual in Morocco. Someone to show her what she didn't do when her father died, guide her in remedying this lapse.

The land here is angry with Monique, too. She left Morocco without doing things properly. Now that she's an adult, she must right these wrongs.

I understand now. I understand. I must help Monique. Show her what she doesn't know, reveal to her exactly what she must do. For her father. For herself. And for this land.

There are no more tears on Monique's cheeks, but she's still crying. I see it.

She's lost in life and believes that returning to Morocco will help her find her taste for it and her direction once again.

Khadija says that Monique never got used to France. She doesn't understand France, Maman. Her country is Morocco.

Her land is Morocco?

She was born here, I know. I know. But even so, someone must speak to her frankly, directly. Monique, you came back here for your father and for yourself. And us? Where are we in you? Who are we to you? Do we even exist somewhere in your thoughts?

Someone must tell Monique what to do. There are things that she can't do here anymore. Despite the authorization of the government and of the king of Morocco, there are things she can't do here anymore as she did before. It's not possible now. Nostalgia for Morocco doesn't justify everything. She must see us, too. Simply take a girl, for example, and turn her into a docile, submissive little maid and an excellent cook—no. No. I know that she'll find another Khadija here with no problem. I know that for sure. I can't do anything about that. But my daughter Khadija, so beautiful, mine—no. Do you hear me, Monique?

Khadija, *laa*. No.

She heard me loud and clear. She's not crying anymore.

I must help Monique.

Even in the shade, near the pond of sacred eels, it's too hot now. I'm sweating again. My body is soaked with sweat.

I look around me. There's no one in Chellah, only me and Monique. I take off the hood of my djellaba. I take off my black veil. I stand up. I walk toward the pond. I take a bit of cool water. I wash my face and my arms. Aaaaahhh, *alhamdolillah*! Praise be to God.

I see an eel emerge from its cave at the very bottom of the pond and approach me very slowly. Its way of moving through the water captivates me immediately. And I have the impression that it's speaking to me. Yes, this eel speaks:

Malika, you are the first woman to come here today. I'm hungry. Did you bring me something to eat?

From my sirwal pocket, I take out a hard-boiled egg. I remove the shell quickly. I split it into four large pieces. I throw them into the pond. I make a wish.

Khadija. Khadija. Khadija.

If the eel eats the egg, the entire egg, the wish will come true. That's what the legend and the ancestors say.

The spirits of the ancestors never lie.

I watch, I wait.

The eel swims around the pieces of my egg without touching them.

I don't pray. My heart is calm. Everything depends on the sacred eel now. The future will be decided, written here, before my trusting eyes.

Something isn't right. The eel swims away without eating my egg. It heads back to its cave. Bad luck. Bad luck. Bad luck.

The eel is in its cave. I can't see it anymore. My heart is beating rapidly.

What did I do wrong? Was I too harsh, too intransigent with Monique? What was my mistake? That I brought a non-Muslim to this sacred, secret place?

I place my hand over my heart. I think it's stopped beating.

I turn to Monique. She's still sitting on the stairs. Her back hunched. Her head in the palm of her hand. She is somewhere else. She is daydreaming. She is still sad. At an impasse. The same impasse as me? No. Of course not.

But maybe I'm wrong. Monique is here, in the same place as me, in the same inferno, in the same mystery.

Monique and Malika.

The borders and battles come to a halt. The past is erased. Everything is suspended. There is only this moment, stripped bare, that counts.

Malika and Monique, momentarily outside of the world and its unjust logic.

I am forced to bow before this force that speaks to me through the sacred eel.

I am nothing before destiny.

I call her. Monique. She doesn't hear me. Monique! Monique! She lifts her head. She seems surprised. Without the hood and veil, she doesn't recognize me, I think.

Malika. *Ana* Malika. I am Malika.

She stands up. She doesn't move. She keeps staring at me.

I turn to the sacred pond. I see two eels preparing to emerge from their hiding place. They move very slowly toward the four large pieces of my egg.

They find them. They eat them.

Monique joins me. She sees what I see in the pond. The realization of my wish?

I thank God. I thank the spirits. I imagine Khadija next to

me. I take Khadija in my arms. I kiss her, my Khadija. You are my daughter, you are my daughter. Mine. Ours. And I let her go.

The eels have eaten everything. But they stay there. They swim in circles. They graze each other. They caress each other. They love each other. They're still hungry.

From my other sirwal pocket, I take out a second egg. I remove the shell. I give it to Monique. I don't explain anything to her. I can't find the words.

Monique takes the egg, without hesitating. She breaks it into several pieces. She throws them to the bottom of the pond.

Did she make a wish? Does she know that she's supposed to make a wish?

The two eels head for the pieces of egg. Snatch them before they've even hit the bottom of the pond. They eat them quickly, very quickly. And they go back to caressing each other.

I look at Monique. She's already looking at me. She's always one step ahead of me. The duel between us will surely begin again. But I no longer have the strength. Neither does Monique. I said what I had to say. Monique listened.

Khadija, *laa*. No.

And, generously, I offer her instead this magical and restorative moment, the baraka, the blessing, of the sacred eels. It doesn't matter what Monique thinks of it all, of this ritual, of the truth that has just been written before us and which will be revealed to us only later. Regardless of her perspective. Let Monique think what she wants about me, about us, let her judge me harshly if she feels like it. Let her laugh at me and the other illiterate, sorcerer Moroccans like me, if that helps her to live. I've already forgiven her.

I forgive you, Monique, and I distance myself from you.

I don't have the words in French to tell her my history, my past, my misery. Tell her about Allal in Indochina, transformed into a killer in Indochina. Reveal to her my own wounds. The impossible mourning of the bled, Béni Mellal. The love stolen away. The life brought to an end when it has only just begun.

Monique doesn't have all the Arabic words.

We're still in the Chellah ruins. There will be no duel. In today's Morocco, it's Monique who wins and will continue to win. I want only one thing: for her to keep her distance from us. I know that she genuinely thinks she's helping me by seeking a relationship with me and Khadija. But no. Absolutely not.

I am here. I took the path all the way to Chellah to tell her to give it up. To leave us alone.

Monique has lowered her eyes. She has understood. She accepts. She lifts them again.

She smiles by way of goodbye. A brief, disappointed, sad smile, which I don't return.

She leaves.

I watch her slowly climb the small staircase.

She has left the shade that protected us. She walks in the scorching mid-afternoon sun, under its murderous blaze. She heads for the large gate of Chellah. Leave. Go. Depart. Vanish. I will never see her again. Phew! What a relief! I will never see Monique again. Pheeewww! It was a dream, a threat that never existed.

Monique falls. Her body collapses.

The sun has assaulted her. A sharp blow that, as if from a finely sharpened blade on Aïd-al-Kabir, the Feast of the Sacrifice, splits open your head and smashes everything inside.

Monique is on the ground. She really fell. I can't believe it. This isn't what I want. This isn't what I wish for her. To die.

A body abandoned on the ground. The body of a very beautiful and very white woman. On the ground. Surrendered to the sun. A body that has another light now. Yellow. Yellow-black.

There is only me. Witness to this fall. To this collapse. There is only me to help her, save her. You were too harsh with her, Malika. Stubborn and intractable as always, Malika. As if your heart were dead. Monique is on the ground, on the ground. She's dying. Do something.

I don't move.

I watch this spectacle. I see it again. Monique staggers slowly: she stops walking, she puts both hands on her head, she lifts her eyes to the sky, she falls. She falls. Falls. She didn't have time to turn toward me. To call for my help. Tell me goodbye. Entrust me with one final message.

I stare. I don't move. Another Malika in me is thrilled. She has achieved her vengeance.

You're wrong. You're wrong. It's not entirely Monique's fault. She was born here, in Morocco. She didn't choose this. She has a right to cling to this land as you do. As you do, Malika.

The storks, everywhere in Chellah, start to clatter. They make love. They mate. They pursue life, a life different from ours. They're noisy and shameless. They don't see Monique lying on the ground. Dying.

The storks now soar through the sky. They do a dance. They conceal the sun. Maybe they'll eat Monique.

I'm afraid.

Monique. Monique!

I stand up. I run, I run.

The world is completely dark now. The storks have made the sun disappear. They're rapturous. They continue to clatter.

Death. The odor of death now descends upon us. I run. I hurtle down the small staircase. I run. I fly. I don't want her to die. I'm not so angry at her that I want harm to befall her. I run. I see her from afar, I get closer and closer. She doesn't move. Her body is still. I run. Even now, under threat, how beautiful she is! I run. Her chest. I run and I concentrate on Monique's chest. I can't see. Finally I see. Her chest rises and falls. It rises again. It falls again. She's not dead. She's not dead. I run. The sun is still obscured by the storks. Chellah is black. I run. Monique. Monique! I yell. Monique! She doesn't answer. I run. *Monique!*

I'm on the ground, next to her. I put my ear to her heart. It beats. Thump. Thump. Thump. I hear it. It beats. Thump. Thump. Thump.

I place my hand on her face, on her forehead. Her skin is burning.

Monique is unconscious.

I know that I shouldn't shake her head to wake her up, that it could be dangerous.

I look at the trees around me. There's a eucalyptus tree. I go toward it. I touch it. I kiss it. I encircle it with both arms. I ask its permission. I cut a few leaves. I return to Monique who is gone from the world.

I rub the eucalyptus leaves between my hands. Their fragrance, fresh and powerful, rouses her. I bring them to Monique's nose so that she breathes in this freshness that brings the dead back to life. I know this will work.

Monique opens her eyes. Immediately.

I'm here, Monique.

I help her get up, carefully.

We stand.

The sun is back with us, on us, triumphant, arrogant, and always merciless.

The storks have disappeared. It's as if they weren't here just a minute ago.

We walk, Monique and I. We head to the pond of sacred eels. It's the only place I can bring her to take care of her as best I can and protect her from the sun.

We descend the small staircase.

I lay Monique on the ground.

With both hands, I take some cool water from the pond.

I wash Monique's face. I wash Monique's hands. Her arms. Her feet. Her eyes. Her nape. Her lips.

Monique watches me. She lets me do it. She says nothing. There's nothing to say. We mustn't say anything.

I don't want her to die.

Monique and I, without meaning to, have awoken an invisible power that is greater than us and which, like me, perhaps sought to take revenge.

Monique understands, too. Something bigger has arisen. The ancient spirits of the site, of the sacred pond, of Chellah, of the ruins.

We must wait. In silence.

Monique looks at me. Her eyes say it all. Solitude. Distress. Life's traps. And, of course, her father's death, her father's grave in Rabat. No longer knowing which way to go. Where to walk. Everything is heavy. Everything is heavy.

Monique asks my forgiveness. I didn't expect this from her.

I look at Monique. My eyes say it all, too. Insist. I repeat myself. You know nothing about me, Monique. I'm not asking you for anything. Rest. Sleep a while. I won't do you harm. I'm here.

Khadija, no. *Laa.* That's all.

There is no more animosity now, no potential duel. We are equals. That's what I've wanted since the day you went to my house in my absence. That's why I asked Monique to meet me here. *Kif-kif.* No difference. Under the same sun. In the same light.

I see in Monique's eyes that she hears me. She heard me.

With the water from the pond, I wash my hands, my forehead, my neck.

I sit on the steps. Next to Monique. I put the hood of my djellaba back over my head. I put my black veil back over my face.

Monique is on the ground.
We wait together.
It's war and it's peace.
It's peace and it's war.
Someone has just died.

3

Salé

*

I'VE KNOWN THE TRUTH FOR YEARS. YOU'RE like my son Ahmed. You two are the same person. You're alike. In every way. He left. You're still here . . . Don't look at me like that, with those harsh eyes. Those eyes aren't you. And I'm really not afraid of you. Your name is Jaâfar. Isn't it? You're Milouda's son, from City Block 10? . . . Yes, it's you. I'm alone in the house. Alone for years, years now. They all left me. You can take what you want. Steal what you want. No need to threaten me. Lower it, lower that knife. I won't resist. I won't scream. Take. Take. Steal. Steal. They're just things, objects. I have no jewelry. You want money? What do you want? You're like my son Ahmed. You're the same age, I think. Ahmed and you, I know. You don't need to be ashamed in front of me. The truth. Drop the knife. Drop it. It's really you, Jaâfar, Milouda's only son. Am I wrong? . . . You just got out of prison. Zaki Prison, nearby. I don't dare ask what it was like inside that prison. Behind those high walls right in the center of our neighborhood, Hay Salam. I won't ask you questions about that. Don't worry. Before, on the land where they built the prison, you all used to play soccer almost every day. A group of you would organize tournaments against the teams from the Hay Al-Inbiath and Bettana neighborhoods.

And then, without consulting anyone, they raised the walls
of the prison in the middle of our neighborhood, right in
the middle. They had no shame. And you all moved from
the soccer field to the prison cells. So quickly. Everything
happened overnight. A prison for our children, our sons, our
men. No one protested. The government, the *makhzen*, is so
powerful . . . But even so, this was brazen. They constructed
a prison for us right in the middle of us. Not far away, no no.
Our children go directly from their high-school classes to the
suffocating cells of Zaki Prison. It's the same path. To go to
the high school, you have to walk along Zaki Prison, with
its enormous gate. Its terrifying gate. You were there, Jaâfar,
inside those walls. I'm sorry, Jaâfar. I'm sorry. Take what you
want from this house. Steal. Steal. I won't say anything to the
police. But lower the knife, please. You're like my son. You are
my son, too. When I passed by the prison walls I thought of
you, I prayed for you. Words of prayer I had said again and
again but which, addressed to you and the other prisoners,
sounded true, new. Words newly associated with you that
overwhelmed me more than I would have liked. I would cry
sometimes next to the walls of that prison. We bring children
into the world and, just a few years later, at fifteen, twenty,
they end up in prison. Devoured by the makhzen and their
police. And by the time they leave, they're already washed up.
There's no more hope. I know. We call them "the children
of the prison." Life ends so quickly. It's atrocious, it's cruel!
You are not the criminal, Jaâfar. It's them. Them. Go on, take
what you want from my home. Steal. Steal. Here's the refrig-
erator. I just bought it. I'll open it. Look. Look. There are
vegetables inside. There's fruit. Mandarins. Do you like mandarins? Two bananas. Do you like bananas? And the rest of
the tajine from this afternoon. Do you want it? Shall I serve
you some? It's a very simple tajine: chicken with onions and

raisins. Do you like this kind of tajine? Look at me . . . Your
eyes tell me yes, that you like this kind of tajine. Good. Good.
You must be hungry. Let me serve you. A bit of food in your
mouth, in your stomach, will calm you down. You'll see
things in another light afterwards. Okay? . . . You don't want
it. What is there for us to do, then? How is your mother,
Milouda? Have you seen her since you got out of prison? You
shouldn't be mad at her, Jaâfar. What else could she do? She
really didn't have a choice. Your father was dead, you were in
prison. She was still relatively young: forty-five years old. She
remarried. A new man, before it was too late. Don't be too
angry at her, please. It's him, the new husband, who stopped
her from visiting you. It's not her fault. Forgive. Forgive. She's
your mother, no matter what happens. Forgive. Where do
you live? Where do you sleep? Over there, in prison, were
you able to protect yourself? They didn't hurt you too badly, I
hope. I know the stories. I hear the stories. Nights in prison.
The top dogs. The little guys. What they force you to do at
night. Come to my arms. Drop that knife and come. Your
eyes say it all. All. My God, my God, life is so unjust, unjust, so
very unjust. Come, Jaâfar. I don't want you to go back to prison.
Come. I'll give you what you want. Come. You're like Ahmed,
I know. The same gestures, the same mannerisms. That must
not have made things easy for you, in prison. Boys like you
and Ahmed, they insult you, throw rocks at you, at night they
lower your pants. I know. I know all about it. I live in the same
world as you. I know that this is why Ahmed left for France.
He's angry at me, Ahmed. For good reason. I saw what they
did to him. The rapes. All kinds of violations. And I didn't protect him. I did nothing. Said nothing. My son Ahmed, Jaâfar.
My son. I didn't lift a finger. My son Ahmed, Jaâfar. Come to
my arms, Jaâfar. You're like him. Come, come. Eat. We'll eat
this tajine together. Chicken with onions and raisins. It was his

favorite. Come, Jaâfar. Don't kill me, Jaâfar. I'll give you whatever you want . . . Money? Okay. Okay. And much more than
money. Okay. Okay.

The jewels too, Malika. I want your gold. Your gold.

I only have a very old gold bracelet, Jaâfar. It's not worth
anything now.

And at the bank? Do you have savings?

Don't be a fool, Jaâfar. People in the street will be alarmed
if they see us walking together. Everyone in the neighborhood
knows that you just got out of prison. Everyone. If we go to
the bank together, they'll arrest you. Let's stay here, in the
house. Have something to eat. And then I'll tell you what I
have in mind. A plan. I have a plan for you and for Ahmed.

I'm not hungry. Say what you have to say, old lady.

I'm not that old, I'm only sixty-five. A widow for just four
years. And then, that's what caused—

Stop messing with my head.

I'm like your mother, Jaâfar.

You're not my mother, old lady. I have no mother. I hate my
mother. Where do you hide your money? Where?

The tajine is really quite good. I'll heat it up. Ahmed always
said that I was a good cook. He loved, adored my cooking.
Why did he go to France? What does he eat in France? What
do people eat in France?

And your gold? Your gold, where do you keep it hidden? In
the cushions in the living room?

Ahmed got used to France, to Paris. So fast. So fast . . . He
doesn't call me anymore. He never answers when I call.

In what cushion, Malika? Tell me! Come with me to the
living room.

Every day, I go to the call shop next door, the one owned by
Mourad, Naïma's son. I give him the little slip of paper where
I've written down Ahmed's French telephone number. He dials

the number while saying each digit aloud.

Are you hiding the gold in this cushion here? Answer me!

Mourad says: No one's picking up, Malika. It's ringing. Ringing. No one's picking up. I ask him to try again: Please, Mourad. Please.

Tell me which cushion your gold is in, or else I'll rip them all up with this knife. Do you understand?

There's still no one picking up, Malika. Mourad's words have become the refrain of my life for the past few weeks now. No one's picking up.

I don't give a shit about your story! I want your money. The gold.

I know it by heart now, Ahmed's French telephone number.

I don't give a shit, I already told you! Tell me which cushion you hide your valuables in. I'm out of patience. I'm pissed off now! I'm pissed off!

00 33 1 45 82 20 35.

I resisted everything in prison, but now I'm on edge all the time. I'm about to explode. I'm warning you, Malika. I won't be able to control myself much longer. Tell me. Tell me! Which cushion? Tell me, you old hag. Tell me!

00 33 1 45 82 20 35.

I have nothing left to lose. Going back to prison doesn't scare me. And this knife, I have to use it on someone: it cost me thirty dirhams.

And one day, it stops ringing. It's not ringing anymore, Mourad said. I'm sorry. I'm sorry. It says: Number no longer in service.

This knife is nice and sharp. It might not be very big, but it's extremely sharp. I sharpened it myself. Look at it. How it gleams. It gleams. Tell me which cushion. You have thirty seconds to answer.

It doesn't ring anymore. It's been disconnected. There's no line between us anymore. Ahmed is lost. He doesn't exist anymore. He's changed numbers. He doesn't answer anymore. But I still go to Mourad. He explains the situation to me in words I don't understand. I beg him: Try again, try, my son Mourad. You never know. Try.

You have fifteen seconds left, Malika. The gold is in which cushion?

It's ringing into the void. No–sorry. It's not even ringing. Number no longer in service. I'm sorry, Malika. You'll have to wait for him to call you and give you his new number. Do you understand?

Five seconds, Malika.

Ahmed is in France. He lives over there. He walks and walks over there. He's in the void. What is France, exactly?

Which cushion? This is your last chance. Answer me, old lady. Answer me!

00 33 1 45 82 20 35.

Your last chance, I said.

This is all that's left to me of Ahmed: a number I know by heart, which is useless now.

Do you hear me, Malika? The cushion, the cushion!

Where is France, Jaâfar? And Paris? It's past Tangiers, is that right? And there's the sea, too.

Speak. Speak! It's like you've gone mad, Malika. Are you not afraid of my knife? Look at it. And now, look me in the eyes.

I have a plan, I told you, Jaâfar. A real plan. And you, you'll help me to accomplish it. Find Ahmed. Bring back Ahmed, Jaâfar. Do you hear me?

And you, do you hear me, Malika? Which cushion?

There's almost nothing in the cushions. Everything is at the bank. I'll save you, Jaâfar. That knife, it's not your future. You're not a killer, I know it. Don't act like a tough guy, it doesn't suit you. It's the last one. The last cushion. The one closest to the living room door. You won't find much in there. Just the gold bracelet. My *chartla*. It comes from very far away, this chartla. It's all I have left of him. Allal. Allal. Allal, before . . . My first husband. He died in Indochina.

What is Indochina?

It's a country at the other end of the world. Where exactly? I don't know. I know only that it takes weeks by boat to get there. One month, two months, perhaps.

I found it, your chartla. This is the chartla that Allal gave you? This is gold? It doesn't look like it, Malika. It seems very old. This isn't gold.

It's gold, I told you. Allal wanted to be with me. He wouldn't have given me a fake chartla. He loved me. This chartla is real, real. Don't call it fake, Jaâfar. It's real. Don't be cruel. Don't destroy my memories. Don't trample on my dreams, please.

This chartla is fake, completely fake! It's worthless. Allal didn't care about you.

Give it to me then, since it's not worth much, as you say. Give it back to me.

Where are you hiding the rest? The other jewels. In which cushion?

Everything is at the bank. How many times do I have to tell you? Was it cold in prison? Did you get used to prison quickly? Did you find a protector? Who? A good man? A real man? A bad man?

Stop. Stop talking about that! I have a knife. Don't you see it? Aren't you afraid? The money, which cushion?

They abused you in prison. I see it in your face now. I hear it in your wavering voice.

Watch it. I don't waver, Malika. Never. I'm a man. No one touched me in prison. I asserted myself. From day one. No tenderness in my eyes. Only hard stares, always hard. I yelled instead of talking. That's the only thing that works. I yelled cutting words, spewed filth. Always. I'm a man. And stop talking

to me about Ahmed. I don't really remember your son . . .
Ahmed . . . He was a sissy. A wimp who thought he was a big
shot because he read books. Books!

Do you want something to eat, Jaâfar? The chicken tajine,
with onions and raisins. Come. It's really delicious. Come.
We'll heat it up. Curse the devil and come. Let your blood cool.
Drop the knife. And come. I'm like your mother. You shouldn't
pretend to be something you're not with me.

Stop with the sweet talk.

Come, come eat.

Watch it! You better watch it, Malika. I'm not lying, it's the
truth.

Yes, it's the truth. I know. But come eat.

Five years. It was horrible, in prison. Five horrible years. Horrible. Horrible! They did everything to me. They all took their
turns on me, in me. With their pricks. All of them. The whole
prison. Even the guards. From day one. Even those who knew
me on the outside. Jawad. Ali. Ismaël. Youcef. Kader . . . They
turned against me. They all took advantage of me. Of my ass.
And all the rest. Five years. Najat. That's the first female name
they chose for me.

The tajine, I'll go heat it up. Follow me into the kitchen.
Follow me. And speak. Speak. It will do you good. Speak.

Jaâfar Najat. Najat Jaâfar. Najat . . . Najat . . . I resisted in the
beginning, I cried, and then, one day, I accepted it all . . . It was
a Friday . . . Najat of Zaki Prison. The free whore for the whole
Zaki Prison. Even the bourgeois prisoners, the ones from good
families, wanted me. And even they didn't pay. Najat is here for
everyone. Working boy. Working girl. Sometimes they gave me
fruit: apples, strawberries, mandarins. The prison warden himself had me come into his office. He'd heard talk of me and my
reputation. He wanted to see with his own eyes who this Najat
was. He said nothing to me. He stared at me for a long time

with red eyes, so excited was he by my presence. He locked the door. He lowered the window shade. And he dropped his pants and underwear. I didn't keep him waiting. He was the director. The boss. The *makhzen*. Allah the All-Powerful. I took off my clothes and walked toward him. After, he gave me a kilo of medlars. Medlars. Can you believe it, Malika? Medlars! This is my favorite fruit, he said. They're expensive. And you deserve it, Najat. You really are good, Najat. What's your name? Your real name? Jaâfar, sir. When he summoned me the second time and dropped his pants and underwear, he said: I won't call you Najat. I'll call you Jaâfar. It's a beautiful name. He gave me a kilo of Mirabelle plums that second time. And the third time, an enormous pineapple. It's yellow on the inside, he said. I only like yellow fruits, Jaâfar. You are my yellow fruit, Jaâfar. There is only you, Jaâfar. He said those words to me so many times: You are my yellow fruit. So, so many . . . and . . . and . . . And one day I fell for him. Fell in love with him. I think. It happened in the middle of the night. He was still in his office. He called for me. When I entered, I found him ready. He was naked, already. And his eyes were very red, as always. He put a white sheet on the ground. He lay down on it. Completely naked. He signaled for me to join him. He took off my clothes. I lay down next to him. We did the deed. Sex and everything else. And he told me to stay. We spent the night together, in his office. Fortunately, it was very warm. The next morning, he gave me a kilo of very ripe pears. I ate them all in front of him. All. I was very hungry. He watched me, delighted. He said nothing. Then I dared ask him a question: What's your name? He didn't answer and, for a few seconds, I regretted having been so bold. He kept staring at me. For a long time. A minute or two. And then I realized that he liked it, this new boldness. He was prolonging his pleasure. I said: There's no more fruit, no more pears, I devoured everything. He said: My name is T'Hami. A very beautiful name. T'Hami. T'Hami.

Yes, Jaâfar. It's very beautiful, T'Hami.

I opened the door of his office to leave. And just before I walked out, he said: What fruit do you want for next week? It was a test. Obviously I had to choose a yellow fruit. I thought for a minute. I said: Mangos. I've never eaten one. Mangos are very expensive. And they're not even sold here, in our neighborhood of Hay Salam. Maybe in downtown Salé. But maybe not even there. In Rabat, yes, you can find mangos. There are customers over there with the money to buy mangos.

And you liked them, the mangos? What did they taste like?

I don't know, Malika. The next week, the director didn't summon me. Maybe he's sick, I thought. But no. He forgot about me. That's all. He removed me from his life when he saw that I could speak to him, ask him questions. When he saw in my eyes the love that I had for him. Jaâfar had fallen in love with T'Hami. That wasn't exciting for him. Everything in me was exposed. I was no longer exciting. He had tasted Najat and had made Jaâfar fall in love. Goodbye, Jaâfar. Farewell. I didn't exist anymore. Still in prison but without the director's protection. Back to square one. I had his heart. The heart of a man. If only I hadn't loved him. Men are cruel everywhere, beyond the walls, behind the walls, within the walls. Everywhere. Watch out, don't fall in love anymore, my heart: that's what I told myself again and again. In my ears, T'Hami would sing AbdelHalim Hafez.* The song "Ahwak." "I love you, *ahwak*, and I hope to forget you. Forget my soul with you. And if I lose it, it doesn't matter. In finding you again, I find the world, life. I find them and I forget them. I love you, *ahwak*, and I hope to forget you. Forget my soul with you. In you, *ya* Jaâfar . . ." I believed him. Hearing those words in prison—in prison—touched a part of me that I didn't even know existed. I believed him, T'Hami. And later,

---

* The great Egyptian musician who died in 1977, one of the most popular singers in the world.

in the restless quiet of the night, I remembered those words. My AbdelHalim Hafez. His voice is still in me. Even here, now, standing before you, Malika. I hear him. T'Hami singing and upending everything in me. "*Ahwak* . . . I love you . . . *Ahwak*, Jaâfar . . ." Happiness and hell at the same time. Everything opens and, a second later, everything closes again.

But what happened, Jaâfar? Why did he stop calling you into his office?

He replaced me. Just like that. End of story. T'Hami replaced me with another prisoner. A new prisoner. With very white skin. A guy from the Rif, from Tetouan. His name is Tammam. He's handsome, Tammam. Very handsome and very white. Next to him, I'm just kind of charming. Jaâfar can't compete with Tammam. No one can rival the beauty of people from the north, especially those from Tetouan. They have everything. White, white skin. Incredibly chic accents when they speak Moroccan Arabic. And their gestures, mannerisms, attitudes . . . Tammam pushed me out of T'Hami's heart . . . What a funny name, Tammam! It's not even a Moroccan name, I think. It comes from over there, far away, the Gulf countries . . . And yet Tammam is Moroccan. As Moroccan as you and me. He's handsome. He's beyond handsome. And that protected him from day one. The other prisoners didn't dare harm him, enter his bed at night, do things to him, court him, offer him fruit. No. He was very protected. By the director, by the guards, and by other important people who visited him in prison, quite often. No one dared give him a female name. "Tammam" sounds like someone who has power, someone who has strong support everywhere. A son from an important family. He doesn't come from a rich family, but his beauty has something bourgeois about it. And that was enough. He was untouchable. Reserved ahead of time for those who really matter. The directors. The ministers. The top dogs. And probably others who run this country and crush its citizens day and night. Contrary to what they say, those men at the top of society, they devour boys, too. Women are too easy for them, almost boring. They need some variety from time to time. Difficulty. Another kind of romanticism. Risk that's somewhat risqué. They need a crazy little thing like Tammam who throws them into a panic and puts oil in their knees, as we say, they're so excited. A girl-boy. A boy who is entirely a boy but inhabited, possessed, by the soul of a girl. Tammam is like that. In prison. Outside of prison. Tammam from Tetouan . . . It's funny, isn't it Malika? You can laugh. Laugh. Laugh. I won't ever eat mangos. I loathe mangos.

No, I don't want to laugh at you and your misfortune, Jaâfar. No. I laughed at my son Ahmed and what they did to him. I won't make the same mistake with you. I brought Ahmed into this world, into this life, and I abandoned him. I abandoned him to the others. Those sexually frustrated men, the famished men of the neighborhood. I let them abuse him, rape him, devour him . . .

Why didn't you do anything, Malika? What I said before about Ahmed isn't true. He wasn't nice all the time, but he wasn't cruel . . . You knew, then. You saw it. You watched the men around here rape him and you turned a blind eye. Your son . . .

It was as if I weren't living in the same society as those men of Salé. I don't even understand that word sometimes— "society." Deep down, I thought that to protect myself from all the harshness of this world I had to ignore what they, the others, call "society." I don't recognize their society. I am not society. We are not the society that they want us to be. Intuitively, I constructed something different. This family. My family. And I didn't give a shit about what happened in society. Their society will never be mine. And Jaâfar, I was busy, very busy, all those years. I had to save them all, the whole family. My husband Mohammed who never took initiative. My six girls. My three boys. I had to think of the future for them and for me. Consider the possibilities around me. The worthless possibilities left to the poor. And decide on my own. Impose my decisions on all of them, the whole family. It was in their interest, even if they didn't see it at first. We had to leave the two tiny rooms that they gave us at the National Library in Rabat. They told us to leave. Move. Get out! Leave! But go where? We went to live in Salé. We sold everything we could and bought a house in the Hay Salam neighborhood of Salé. House is actually not the right word to describe what they wanted to sell us. It was one bedroom, a kitchen, and a bathroom. The rest of the house was unfinished. We had to build it ourselves. It took years. Years with all eleven of us in a single bedroom. Eleven. Eleven! I saved cent by cent. I saved everything I could. Some months, I made just one meal a day. They moaned. They shouted. We're hungry! We're hungry, Maman! I didn't have a choice. We needed to save more and more. They all thought I was merciless. Oh well. One day, they would understand the sacrifices I made for them. The humiliations I endured because of them, to give them a roof, a house. A real house. This house you're in now, Jaâfar. A house with three floors. It's worth a lot of money today. This house, you see, I built it on my own. Built it wall after wall. Floor after floor. It was a huge ordeal, all of it. A war. I was alone. I didn't have the time really to see Ahmed, to understand him completely, to protect him or to defend him. Ahmed wasn't the only one. I have nine children. He's the eighth. The others had taken everything, all my energy and attention. I had to choose who among them to love the most. It wasn't Ahmed. I admit it. I gave more, more, to my eldest son. Slimane. That's just how life is. You have to set your priorities. I set myself a goal: Build the house. Negotiate firmly with the masons. Beg the civil servants of the administration to give me the building permits even though I couldn't afford them. Kiss their hands and feet. Bribe the police officers when they showed up at our house to stop construction. Cry in front of them and promise them a nice couscous once a week for two months straight. I did all of that, Jaâfar. Alone. Alone. Does Ahmed remember this? Does he at least know this? No. Of course not. And during all this time, I also had to deal with the hostile world around us. Society. Their society. Keep away the jealous, mean, dangerous, wretched neighbors who did everything to stop me in my tracks. Battles every day. The house. This is what will save them all later on. Over the years, these walls will be worth money, a lot of money. One day, they'll thank me. A big, sincere thank you. For now, they have all abandoned me. They want to be free of me, they say. Make their own families. They will return. They will return. When I'm dead. And they will understand. Even Ahmed will understand. For now, he doesn't even answer the phone. France swallowed him up. Devoured him. I'm not lying. I only have the old number: 00 33 1 45 82 20 35. It's not valid anymore. But that doesn't surprise me. Ahmed was always a little bit mean. A little bit cold. His sisters had a nickname for him: the Heartless One.

Ahmed, heartless! He's your son, after all, Malika . . .

He's my son. But he doesn't answer the phone. He chose France.

You're just like my mother, Malika. You talk like her. You did nothing for Ahmed. And that's why he turned mean, cold, as you say. That's the only explanation.

He didn't even consult me when he made the decision to go to France. He asked me for money. But I gave him nothing. He made his bed. Let him lie in it to the end. I wasn't about to give him the bit of money I'd managed to save over the years . . . He's not the only one. There are his brothers and sisters, too. And there are eight of them. They live their lives. They're married. They have children. I've done more than my duty toward them. And I don't want them to come to see me too often. There's always some new complaint. I don't recognize myself in them. It's like they inherited nothing from me. They're my children, and yet they don't really resemble me. They're a little too accommodating with their spouses. They're afraid of their spouses. And frankly, each time I notice it, I want to laugh. I look at them and I say to myself: This is the end result, my children, the fruit of all those years of sacrifice. I'm disappointed. I don't agree with their decisions and, when I tell them, they're not pleased. Too bad. I'm their mother. I have every right. I say what I want. They get angry. They sulk. They always end up coming back when new problems arise. They all come back. And I have to tell them what to do each time, how to respond, where to go, how to fix things. They still need me when they believe someone has cursed them or looked at them with the evil eye. Then I have to undo the spell, perform a magic ritual to heal them, caress them, coddle them, nourish them, restore them. I'm tired of them. There are eight of them. Eight. And it never stops, their demands, their needs, their weaknesses, their dull moral quandaries. They tire me out. I'm alone in this house, and it's not easy, the solitude, but I'd rather they not invade my space. I've given too much. And when I get scared, all alone in the empty house, I turn on the television and leave it on day and night. I don't turn it off. The sounds and noises fill up the silence and speak to my phantoms . . . You think that I'm a disgraceful mother, a harsh woman, Jaâfar. Is that it? This isn't harsh. How I treat my children now. They have to grow up, that's all there is to it. Grow up far away from me. I tell them the truth, like you did, Jaâfar, when you told me the truth about what happened in prison. Your story interests me. Your life interests me. Them, my children, I know everything about them. I know in advance what they're going to ask me. They devour me. Drain me. They don't see me. You, Jaâfar, you came to my home to harm me, steal from me, hit me, maybe kill me, and yet I see that you listen to me. You see me. You look at me. You don't pretend. You listen to me. Am I wrong? . . . In the end, Ahmed is the only one who resembles me. He was by my side over the years and I didn't see that he was the one who learned the most from me. Now that he's far away, now that he's had the strength and the audacity to cut off ties with me, disappear voluntarily, I see. I finally see. Ahmed is like you, Jaâfar. Ahmed is like me too, like his mother Malika.

You speak of nothing but yourself, Malika. You know nothing about what I've really been through, what Ahmed's really been through. Death every day. Here. All around your three-story house. You said nothing. You let it happen. Ahmed and I shattered each day and raped each day by men you know very well, men who still live here, next door to you, in this evil neighborhood that we call Hay Salam. You're guilty, Malika. You're like my mother. She's the one who sent me into this criminal life. I didn't become like this by accident: a criminal at the age of twenty-two. Prisoner at the age of twenty-two. She is largely, largely responsible for all of this. And when they threw me behind the walls of Zaki Prison, she acted as if I didn't exist anymore. My mother. My mother! And yet the prison is only fifteen minutes from her house by foot. You speak of your son Ahmed and you don't even think of asking his forgiveness. Yes, Malika, forgiveness. Sincerely asking forgiveness. Your only concern is that you're not in control of Ahmed anymore. He's no longer by your side, suffering in silence by your side while you pretend not to know anything about it. Ahmed cut you off, yes, and he was right to do so. Your other children have become an annoyance to you. You need a new one. Is that it? Someone to whom you'll grant the illusion that he can resist you while, deep down, all you do is manipulate him. Like every mother, like every woman, you have a skill for that. Manipulate. Manipulate. Blind the others. You play the role of the abandoned woman perfectly, but it's you who abandoned Ahmed, not the

other way around. I don't know if life is better in France, but
he had a thousand reasons to put all those miles between you
and him, to exile himself on another continent, to enter that
voluntary distance and that unbreakable silence. I'm with him.
Ahmed. I don't know how he managed to find the money to go
over there. I can easily imagine what illegal things he did to get
there—at least, illegal in your eyes, and in the eyes of this cruel
world. I'm with him. When we were teenagers, for two or three
years, Ahmed told me everything, and I told him everything. I
would call him, he would call me. We would meet. We would
walk to the center of Salé. And we would return. Sometimes,
we said nothing. We were just there, side by side. We would cry.
We would both cry in silence. You have to apologize, Malika.
You're his mother. And you have to apologize. You say that you
only have his old number in France. You say that you have no
way to reach him. But I, Jaâfar, I'm here, in front of you. Jaâfar
is Ahmed. Ahmed is Jaâfar. Apologize. Apologize. You're not the
only one suffering in this life, in this world. There isn't only your
version of events. You keep saying again and again that we don't
know everything. Money! I want money. Where do you hide
the money? In the dresser? In the bathroom?

You don't want to eat the tajine, Jaâfar? Let's eat, it'll get cold
again.

Your food isn't good. I don't like it. Too much salt. Too much
pepper. It stings. I still have the sharpened knife in my hand.
Look. Look me in the eyes. The money. Where?

Don't ruin everything, Jaâfar. We'll come to an understanding, you'll see. I have a plan. I'll give you the money you
want. You'll go to France, too.

You're out of your mind, Malika. I don't want to go to
France. I'm not interested. The world, for me, is here.

You will go over there and bring back Ahmed. I have money.
It's in the bank. You'll go to Paris. You'll look for him every-

where. You'll find him. And you'll speak to him, to Ahmed. He will listen to you, I'm sure of it. You will return together. You'll both live with me. Here, in this house that's filling up with more and more phantoms. You'll make a life for me, around me. I will be a mother to both Ahmed and Jaâfar. You will be as you are. I accept you as you are. You don't have to change anything about yourselves. I have a lot of money at the bank. A few thousand dirhams. It's never too late. It's July 1999. Ahmed left just a year ago. Less than a year. You must go over there, speak to him over there, tell him my words and my apologies if you want before he's settled in France for good. It's not too late, no. There's still some hope. How many years do I have left to live? How many? I don't want to die without having accomplished my mission with Ahmed. I want to finally give him what I never gave him. I have time now. That's all I have now: time, endless and empty. Please. Please, Jaâfar. You don't need to rob me. I'll give you what you want. What your mother didn't give you, Jaâfar, I'll give to you myself. Me, Malika.

You'll never be my mother. I don't want a mother now.

I understand what you've been through. I knew what they did to Ahmed. It's true. I have regrets. I live in regret.

You will pay. Where is it, the money? Answer me, quick, quick! Don't try to eat my brain with your words, it won't work. I've already heard it all, seen it all. And Zaki Prison only confirmed my sentiments from the beginning. There's no hope. Barely twenty-seven. Twenty-seven. There's no hope left. You say that you have regrets, Malika, but you don't actually know what I've been through, before prison and in prison. You don't know the details, the traces left on my body. On Ahmed's body. You know nothing. The world set its famished lions on Ahmed, on me, and watched the spectacle: live rapes, live death. You were among the spectators, Malika, and you didn't lift a finger. Your son, you brought him into the world and you sent him to his death. Every day.

You have no heart, Malika. Your regrets today are useless. Absolutely useless. You act as if you have sympathy for me, for my misfortunes. You pretend to be interested in what I went through in prison, but it's only a facade. You say that you want to save me today, but that needed to happen yesterday. Yesterday. Ten years ago. Fifteen years ago. Now that I have my official criminal diploma bestowed by the prison, I refuse your apologies and I will see my career through to the end. Petty criminal to serious offender. And prison doesn't scare me anymore. I know that I'll have to go back one day or another. I have friends there, partners, lovers. Loves. I don't want you to save me. Ahmed was right to go to France. And don't you worry, life made him strong and tough. France is nothing at all, it could never crush someone like him. It's the other way around. Your son Ahmed is intelligent and calculating. He aimed high. For him, the conquest of France and the French! That's where the money is, real money, and you have to be over there to take all that money, to take power and revenge. Revenge against the whole world. Revenge against even this cold and unfeeling earth. Ahmed has only just arrived there, and you already want to stop him, keep him from making progress, from becoming someone. Becoming someone without you. You're not thinking about him. You're thinking only of yourself and your solitude in this house. You're self-centered, Malika. Ahmed died years ago, in front of you, and you did nothing. Your regret is useless. Your regret isn't about Ahmed. Your regret is only about you, you, you. Not him. Not me.

I miss him.

He has his own life to live. Deep down, what scares you is dying. Dying without seeing Ahmed again . . . We're all going to die, Malika. He was in front of you, day and night. Never did you tell him the words that you've just said to me. You said nothing. Like plenty of people around here, in this Morocco full of fear. You're a criminal, too.

I did what I could. France took Allal, my first husband. It killed him in Indochina. France has no right to take my son from me now.

France is just a place with a lot of money. Instead of being abused every day in Morocco without anyone to defend him, Ahmed went over there to take that money. Deep down, that money is his, already his. I have no doubt that the art of survival he mastered in Salé will serve him very well over there. And your stories, your past, your sacrifices, your misfortunes . . . frankly, I don't find that stuff interesting. I wasn't there for that past. I don't see it. I'm here, in the present. Here, now. I just got out of prison. And I need money. Your money. You're old. You've lived your time. You don't need money anymore. I'm twenty-seven. I need money more than you. The money. And who cares if I go back to prison soon? In any case, in the future, serving time in prison won't be considered so shameful in Morocco. Quite the opposite. I'm a pioneer, you see.

Hassan II . . . Hassan II will die. Hassan II is in the hospital. The Avicenne hospital in Rabat. He's on his last legs. Once he's gone, things will be different.

I don't care about that. No one has ever done anything for me, to save me. Not Hassan II or anyone else. You're delirious again, Malika. It's like you don't know Morocco. The system of Morocco. The reality of Morocco. The cruelty of Morocco.

I'm only telling you that there might be some hope . . .

In Hassan II's death?

Maybe.

I didn't think you were this naive.

I'm not naive, Jaâfar. You don't know my whole past. I come from very far away. From the bled. From poverty. From war.

Stop. Stop. All this stuff from the past . . . You've already talked about all that.

That's all I can do now, repeat myself. I have to recount the past, my past . . . I waged war. Several wars. Even if the world was cruel to you, Jaâfar, it was worse to me, worse than anything you can imagine. And despite it all, I, an illiterate woman, achieved this miracle: I saved them all, even Ahmed. All. All. And even if my children aren't grateful today, that's okay. My past and my battles, it's time for them to know. I'm the one who thought of everything, built everything, achieved everything.

You talk like the people on television. Do you want a medal, Malika? Do you want the recognition of the state? Of King Hassan II, before he dies?

Why not? You don't think I deserve a bit of recognition?

I don't give a shit . . . The money. Get up and show me where you hide the money.

But we haven't finished eating the tajine, Jaâfar. It's not right, we must eat everything, and leave nothing for the devil. The devil . . . Help me finish the tajine, please. Drop the knife and eat some more. There might be a bit too much pepper, but it's good anyway. Come. Eat. Eat. It would make me happy to see you eat. That's the only real thing. Eating. Chicken, onions, and raisins will give you energy and put you in a good mood. You'll see. You'll be transformed. Take this piece, the thigh. Do you like the thigh?

I like the breast.

Very good. Here's the breast. I'll eat the thigh myself . . . You don't say thank you, Jaâfar? Okay, then. Eat. Eat. Do you know the French film *Au revoir les enfants*?

No.

I saw it with Ahmed on television, a long time ago. Ever since he left, since he's no longer in this home, I've been thinking of that film. There are two boys, two teenagers, in a boarding school. It's winter. There's snow. It's cold. Everyone is cold. Everyone is afraid. There are Germans, German soldiers. They're onscreen sometimes, not all the time. What we see mostly are the children, the many teenagers . . . Ahmed is there now, and when I try to imagine the reality he lives in, where he works, where he sleeps and who's around him, this film comes to mind.

It's a war movie?

No. I think . . . but I'm not sure . . . There are children in hiding, two or three, among others. They're in danger. They're Jewish.

France kills the Jews?

There's an empty bed next to the protagonist's bed. They give it to one of those three Jewish children. He's sad and he's brave, that little Jewish boy, it's clear from the start. And he has slightly curly hair. I don't know his name. The hero of the movie, I don't remember his name either.

Why are you bringing this up?

No reason. We're talking. I'm making another connection between you and Ahmed. That's what I see. *Au revoir les enfants* . . . Ahmed lives in a French film . . . At the end, someone informs on the three Jewish children. The German soldiers enter the school. They arrest them and the priest who's been protecting them. All the children are in the big schoolyard. Everyone is cold and afraid. Just before leaving, disappearing completely, the priest turns back to the children and says calmly: *Au revoir, les enfants* . . . They all answer: *Au revoir, mon père*. I don't speak French. Ahmed explained it to me. And then . . . then . . . nothing. The hero says that it's the last time he saw them. The three little Jewish boys. The priest was very kind. They died. All four of them dead. Jaâfar, you must go over there and bring Ahmed back. How many years do I have left to live? Five? Ten? Fifteen? The others are here beside me. But Ahmed lives in *Au revoir les enfants*. I have to do something. You don't think so? Bring Ahmed back. That's my role as his mother. I am his mother. I'm finally waking up. The past is the past, Jaâfar. This is today. And I told you that I was sorry. I want to make up for it. Ahmed chose France. I don't agree with his choice.

Ahmed knows better than you what's best for him. He doesn't need your blessing, your help, your opinion. What he did, I would have done too if I'd been in his place. Exile myself. Go far away. That's the only solution. Live at a distance. Live among strangers. Reinforce the solitude rather than trying to push it away. That's the only way. Ahmed won't come back. And I won't go looking for him. Get that into your head, Malika.

One day, Ahmed will wake up, and it will be too late. I won't be here anymore, on this earth. One day, he'll walk alone in the streets of France and he'll understand. He'll see. He'll remember. What I gave him despite everything. What I did for him. He'll see it all. All. And he won't be able to cry because of all his shame at having cut off his mother and let her die without saying to her: I'm sorry, Maman. One day, the years will fall on his shoulders, heavy, exhausting, merciless. And there will be no one by his side over there. He'll grab the phone, he'll dial my number, and at the very last second, he'll realize that I'm no longer here. Malika, dead. Then he'll live the rest of his life in an ocean of regret. On a slow, slow, empty path, to his death . . . Isn't it true, what I'm saying? You know that I'm right, Jaâfar. I'm reaching out my hand to him, to Ahmed.

He changed his number. I'm not going to France, Malika.

Please, Jaâfar. Look—you've just eaten my food. Something of me is in you now. I'm prepared to do anything . . . As long as he forgives me and returns . . . Ahmed . . .

The future is staying over there, in France. He won't return.

The future? What future? Money? Money isn't everything. Life should be lived alongside each other.

For people like Ahmed and me, the future is in France. And stop yelling at me, Malika. You're not my mother. You're acting like some sensitive mother who wants the best for her children, but it's too late. It's too late between you and Ahmed. Has been for a long time already, not only since he left. And you still don't want to acknowledge the harm you've done to him.

What harm? I carried him in my womb. I gave birth to him. I fed him. I cared for him. I raised him. I put him through elementary school, then high school, then university. Does none of that count? All of that is love, dedication, encouragement. Every day he had food to eat. Is that nothing? A mother who wakes up early, makes bread, washes the dirty laundry, cleans the house, prepares food four times a day for eleven people for years on end, is that nothing? You want me to apologize to Ahmed, but what are you talking about, Jaâfar? What should I apologize for? The world has turned upside down. You told me to stop yelling. No. I will yell. I'll yell! Ahmed suffered. But it was worse for me, much worse! They raped Ahmed. But they killed my husband, in Indochina. And I was put out on the street. The street. The bled. Do you understand? The street. Out in the countryside. And now I'm supposed to apologize for not doing more? Never! Over my dead body. I saw what Ahmed was from the start. His nature. But I didn't throw him out. I didn't do that. I didn't do what other parents in Morocco do. I kept him here and I gave him his chance like the others. To eat like the others. I sent him to school. I did all that for him. And now, at twenty-seven years old, he chooses France, he disconnects his phone and acts as if I, his mother, were out of touch, a savage who understands nothing of life, of culture and struggle . . . What a disappointment! How shameful! My son isn't my son anymore. He has severed all connection between us. That's his response. Is that what it means to be modern today? Ignore your mother? Kill your mother? And if he doesn't remember what I gave him, if he doesn't remember my food, let him ask his stomach. Surely Ahmed's stomach has more pity for me than he does. Ahmed has forgotten even the gratitude of his stomach. How tragic . . . He's not my son anymore. He's not my son anymore . . . It's not worth going to France to bring him back, Jaâfar. You're right. He doesn't deserve it. It's over. Over. Let him live in his cold and self-centered freedom over there, without us, without me. He's not my son anymore . . . Do you want my money in the bank? Is that it? How much do you need? Answer me. Do you have a place to live? Do you want to stay here with me? You can, Jaâfar. You can . . . You're not saying anything. Speak . . .

I'm not Ahmed, Malika. I'm not looking for a new mother.

You're a thief, I know.

Exactly. A thief.

And that's why you served time in prison. Who did you steal from?

I went into a villa not far from the center of Salé. Only the man of the house was there. He was a big guy. I didn't manage to steal from him. But we fought. I planted my little knife in his thigh. And even so, he won. He tied me up and beat me all over for an hour. Then he called the police . . . You know the rest. Five years in prison. Attempted robbery and attempted murder, they said . . . At twenty-seven years old, it's already over for me. There's nothing else to do. Keep stealing. That's what my life will be. Theft. Thief.

That's very dangerous, Jaâfar.

I just got out of prison, and over there, it wasn't just dangerous. Every day I could have been killed. Every day I had to negotiate with lions, tigers, and crocodiles. I offered up my ass. As many times as they wanted. It saved me. I'm saved. What else can I do now? Steal. Keep stealing. It's simple. Steal. Steal. And I know that I'll go back to prison soon. I can't wait, to tell the truth. I miss them a lot . . . The lions, the tigers, the crocodiles—Zaki Prison. At least, behind those walls, I don't have to justify anything. Love between men is allowed, facilitated, encouraged. Never punished. They can't do it, punish that love. They know that without it, without that love, prison wouldn't last a single day. There would be a revolt, a revolution, fire, everything ablaze. Since I got out of Zaki Prison, I think of only one thing: taking off again, going back there, reuniting with my friends, my partners, my rapists, my lovers, the rank food, the sounds, the silence . . . Getting a glimpse of the warden, T'Hami, from time to time. I don't hope anymore that he'll take me back one day. I'll think of another strategy to take some small revenge against him, obtain those mangos one day, no matter what—the ones he promised me.

The mangos. You haven't forgotten. Are you serious, Jaâfar? You've lost your mind!

I miss it all. In my head, day and night, I live, I travel, I walk through the hallways and the wings and the cell blocks of that prison. I was there from twenty-two to twenty-seven years old. Nearly five years. There, I learned to forget the outside, build nothing for the outside, make no plans. I got used to the violence of prison. I got used to the rules and the confined space. I was in the D block. I even miss the suffocation and the panic attacks I would feel sometimes. There were sixty of us in the same block. Sixty people in sixty square meters. I dream of finding myself back in the heart of that block, in the middle of those brothermen, in the middle of those renegade bodies. There's nothing left to lose: we're all criminals. The future? What future? We have found our place, our center. Zaki Prison. We don't need to dream anymore. We're bad, officially designated as bad. It's written on our foreheads. Since I got out, everyone in the streets of Hay Salam sees me as an ex-con. Everyone rejects me all over again. Everything is closed. Every door. There's nothing left to hope for. I just want to be back behind the walls. Be with my friends, my brothers, my men. It's war and it's peace. It's peace and it's war. One nested inside the other forever. No respite. Peace in prison has a different taste. War in prison is worthy of being waged. We do it all without hiding ourselves. That's what I miss the most: not hiding. Since I got out, I have to hide again, play several parts at once, be a hypocrite, be strategic, be fake all the time. Have a thousand and one faces. It's not for me anymore. I don't have the codes to this place anymore. I don't understand anything here anymore. My mother isn't my mother now. She's remarried. She's somewhere else, far, far away. And I don't want to find her again. I want to be back among the men of the prison. They are the ones who are free. I know that it's difficult to believe, but in prison we are free. Your son Ahmed went to France. I want to go back there, to the other side of the sun, of life, of the screen, of the stars. And you, Malika, you will help me achieve it. I followed you down the street, I entered your home. I don't really want to steal from you. No. No. You're just going to help me. You'll call the police and accuse me of something terrible. You must, Malika. I want to return to Zaki Prison. Please. Please . . . If you don't do it, I'll be forced to . . . knife in your thigh, like the other guy, the man in the villa. Please . . .

No. Jaâfar. No.

Then you leave me no choice.

Do what you have to do.

You're not afraid, Malika? . . . No? . . . I don't want us to go to the bank. Just give me the money you have here, in your home.

I don't have much here.

Do you want me to cry, Malika? You weren't sufficiently moved by all the tragedies I've just told you? You want more sad stories about my miserable life? How much money do you have? . . . Answer. Look. Get a good look at the knife. It's extremely sharp. Don't make me hurt you. Please. Please.

No.

Then . . . I'll steal from you, Malika, and plant this knife in your thigh so that they sentence me again to at least eight or nine years. It's my only chance. That's the only way they'll put me back in the same exact wing of Zaki Prison. Where my friends are, my loves. They're waiting for me. I miss them . . . No, I'm not crazy. Hurry up, Malika! The money. How much do you have here? How much?

Five thousand dirhams . . . Six thousand.

That's nothing, six thousand. Six thousand dirhams . . . What am I supposed to do with that? The best thing would be to send it as a money order to Marwan, in prison. He'll keep it for me, until I go back. Six thousand . . . You swear, Malika? You don't have any more? God is watching you, Malika. Don't lie. Do you swear?

I swear, Jaâfar.

You'll come see me in prison. Now and then. Not all the time. Just now and then. I'll take my money from you. I'll plant my knife in your thigh. And I want you to come see me, now and then, in prison. We know each other now, Malika. And I've eaten food made by your hands. That counts for something, doesn't it? Don't come too often. Come see me once a year, no more . . . If only to tell me whether Ahmed has gotten back in touch with you or not. That's a good reason.

You're alone in the world.

Not any more than you, Malika.

Prison isn't a life. One day, you'll grow old. You'll get out of prison old, and it'll be far too late. You'll never be able to get used to life on the outside.

You've understood nothing of what I've been telling you for the last hour at least, Malika.

And you, Jaâfar, you've heard nothing of what I told you about Ahmed.

It's over. Time to go. Give me the six thousand dirhams. Where are you hiding them? Where? In your bra? Is that it? . . . That's it . . . Take them out . . . Take them out.

Here it is. The six thousand. A little more, even. Six thousand two hundred dirhams.

Thank you. Thank you. I'll tell my friends in prison about you. I'm serious. I have nothing against you, Malika.

Thank you, Jaâfar.

You're welcome. And now, the knife. I'll plant it in your thigh. It'll be quick. It won't hurt too much. You'll see. Close your eyes if you want. Or you can watch. What do you prefer?

Wait, wait. Do you know how to write in French?

A little bit.

You'll help me write a letter to Monique.

Who's Monique?

When she came back to see me in the mid-eighties, with her two boys, she left me an envelope. There was a bit of money inside. And her address. She lives in Paris. Ahmed is in Paris now. Do you see?

No, I don't. Who's Monique?

She's a French woman who wanted to hire my daughter Khadija as a maid in her villa in Rabat, a very long time ago. But I refused. I did everything to keep Monique away from us, from our lives and our plans. I had big ideas, very big, for Khadija. A beautiful marriage with one of those important men in the ministries or from the royal palace in Rabat. None of that happened. I got it completely wrong. Khadija fell in love with Saïd, a poor mason who worked sometimes in the National Library. Saïd was very handsome. That was his only quality: beauty. And, of course, beauty attracts and demands beauty. He fell in love with Khadija, too. He wanted to marry her. She was only seventeen years old. There was still hope that she would find a rich husband in Rabat who would save us all. Even my husband Mohammed didn't want to follow my lead anymore: You stopped Khadija from going to France with Monique and having a beautiful future, you won't stop her from living a happy life now. Khadija has found love. Saïd is poor but he cares about her.

Did she marry Saïd?

Yes. I made a mistake. Maybe I should have let her go with Monique.

She would have been a maid all her life. Life is more than that. You were right to say no.

Sometimes I regret it.

You're wrong, Malika.

No one helped me. I thought that with a rich man from Rabat, our life would be easier. That we'd have a bit of wealth and comfort, finally. Khadija chose love with a poor man. Saïd. And I had to keep battling. Take care of all of them, feed them, clothe them. And save, cent by cent, to construct this house in Salé. They didn't help me. They didn't make my job easier.

And what do you want me to do about it?

You'll help me, Jaâfar. We'll write a letter to Monique. We'll tell her about Ahmed. We'll tell her the story, just some of it, not everything. We'll tell her that we can't reach him. And we'll ask her to help us find him. They both live in Paris. Paris can't be that big. Right? Monique. Monique. Why didn't I think of her before? She's the one who'll help me. She *must* help me. She *will* help me.

But you refused to let her hire your daughter as her maid . . .

Exactly. Monique liked that I resisted her. And surely she still remembers what happened between us in the Chellah ruins. Of course she remembers.

What happened?

I'll tell you about that another time. When Monique came to see me in the eighties, she went about things the right way. She went to see my husband at his work, at the National Library, and asked him to let me know that she'd be coming to see me in Salé three days later. She didn't just show up at my house out of the blue, as if my home were hers, her territory and her law. No. She knew that she had to show me some respect. She gave me three days' warning. Plenty of time to prepare and clean my house so that I could welcome her properly.

And she came?

Not only did she come but, on top of it, she brought her two boys with her. Young teenagers. Fourteen and twelve. Well groomed. Handsome. Very well mannered. Pierre and Emmanuel. I think Monique wanted to honor me by doing that. She was showing me her children. What was most dear to her. She also wanted to tell me that she hadn't had a daughter. And that she wouldn't have one. She was over forty years old by then. Too late for her to have more children. That was the message.

What message? I don't understand.

Your daughter Khadija could have been my daughter. The daughter that I never had. But you were stronger than me, Malika. I recognize that. And I'm not angry at you. That's what she said.

She speaks Arabic?

Yes, a bit, not very well. But the few Arabic words she knew sufficed to convey her message.

Very direct. What did you say in response?

Monique was in my home, I couldn't attack her. I chose to ignore her message. And I said, to reassure her: To each is written his mektoub. Khadija married a man she loves. That's what she wanted. Khadija says that she's happy. I don't know if I should believe her. She chose love. And her father supported her choice. I said nothing. I did my duty. And I moved on to other things . . . Monique seemed satisfied with my response. She asked me to show her around my home. There wasn't much to show. An unfinished house that lacked nearly everything . . . But a clean house, gleaming with cleanliness. It smelled like the *jaouï* I'd burned before Monique arrived. She said that it was the first time she'd been back to Morocco since what had happened in the Chellah ruins. Her father Georges's grave in the Christian cemetery of Rabat had summoned her once again. She had to answer the call. Visit the grave and introduce her two sons to her father.

But he's dead?

The dead are not merely dead. We have to keep them in our thoughts, live with them, tell them about what happens to us. Maintain this bond until the end. Not let them die completely. Monique said that she really wanted her father to see her two sons. From his grave, love them and take them in his arms, in his breath. I liked that, her way of speaking and believing. I stood up. I went into the kitchen. I prepared a large pot of mint tea. I placed it in front of Monique and her two sons, with three packets of Henry's cookies. Pierre and Emmanuel adored it. They ate all the cookies and drank the whole pot of tea. The sugary mint tea riled them up, they were vibrant and joyous. Monique and I were delighted. She said: They love Morocco, as you can see, Malika. I answered: They are welcome in Morocco. Monique was smiling. She was no longer the bourgeois French woman watching us from on high. She was just a mother, touched by her children who were beginning to love something simple and strong in the country where she was born. She seemed almost grateful. Despite the past that was not really past, I welcomed them into my home even so, properly, very properly, her and her children. I welcomed them without any fuss. Sickly sweet mint tea and three packets of Henry's cookies. That was all I could offer. And that was enough. Just before leaving, she gave me a gift: a scarf. A scarf from Paris. Bright red with a floral design. The flower we see everywhere here, in Rabat, in Salé: red hibiscus. A bright red hibiscus scarf. A bright red hibiscus scarf from Paris. There was almost no other color on the scarf. There was also, I think, among the flowers, a stem, also red, with tiny, light-yellow buds.

Do you still have it, this scarf? Where is it?

In the dresser. You want to see it, Jaâfar? Yes? Follow me, then . . . Here's the dresser. Where is that scarf? . . . Not here. Not here, either. Where? . . . Aaah, here it is! Take it, look,

look, touch, touch. It's so red. Put it around your neck, Jaâfar.
Like that . . . Look at me.

You're not saying anything. Does it look good or not?

That scarf is so beautiful on you, Jaâfar. It's yours now. That
scarf suits you very well. It's strange and it's very beautiful
on you. It's yours. It's yours if you help me write the letter to
Monique.

And did you give Monique a gift too?

Two hundred and fifty grams of jaouï. And I told her that she
should only burn a little bit at a time. A tiny amount of jaouï
is enough to transform an entire house: state of mind, bodies,
hearts, head, blood. It's enough for yourself and for others. I'm
not exaggerating. That's what happens when you do it with a
pure heart. It's possible Monique still has some of that jaouï that
I gave her so long ago now. The older it gets, the better.

Is that jaouï symbolic of something between you and her?

You mean a reconciliation? Let's not get carried away. We
were polite. Courteous. A moment of peace, in the meantime.
That's all. But the past will always be the past. It can never be
forgotten. Do you understand? Take the scarf. It's for you. A
gift. On the condition that you write the letter to Monique.
I still have the letter she sent me after that second visit. Her
address in Paris is on it.

Okay, Malika. I'll do it. I'll take this scarf with me to prison
and I'll give it to Marwan. He'll be thrilled. He loves vibrant
colors. I'll tell him the whole story of this scarf. He'll trust me.
Finally.

And who is this Marwan?

I'll tell you later. Give me a piece of paper and a pen. And an
envelope. Do you have one?

Yes. There must be one among Ahmed's things. They're all
here, in this dresser. Here. Look . . . Yes, look here . . . Did you
find one?

Yes. I have everything. Tell me what you want to say to Monique, and I'll write it in French. Go on.

Dear Monique, hello. It's Malika. Malika from Rabat and Salé. Khadija's mother. I hope that life is treating you and your loved ones well. May God open every door for you and your family. I need you, Monique. Your help. You're the only one who can help me. Only you. And it's because we've gone through intense moments together, you and I, that I dare write to you and make this request of you. Those intense moments were also complicated, difficult moments, I haven't forgotten, but they revealed all my intimate truth before you and all your intimate truth before me. My face in your face. Your face in my face. I write to you today without pretending the battle between us never took place. I only did my duty, you understand, carried out my responsibility. I didn't give Khadija to you, for reasons that you now know very well. When you came to see me in Salé with your boys, Pierre and Emmanuel, I understood that I had your respect. You have mine, too. I was stubborn with you. But I respect you. And that's why I'm writing to you. I respect you. I know that you'll understand my request and my distress. It's about Ahmed, my son Ahmed. Ahmed Kébir. He's twenty-seven years old. He's been in Paris for nearly a year now. And for the last three months, I haven't been able to contact him. He changed his telephone number and he didn't call to give me his new one. He doesn't want to speak to me. He wants to cut off the entire world, me, his family, all of Morocco. He has his reasons, which I understand and which, at the same time, I don't understand. I think he's taking his vengeance on us, on his country, on me above all, because we did nothing to protect him when he was young from the numerous sexual assaults he endured in Salé. Now that he's in Paris, he wants to forget the old world, kiss us goodbye. He's avenging himself. He's avenging himself. He's become harsh, like me. He's become a tiger. A lone tiger. But I'm his mother. His mother, no matter what . . .

Malika, I think you have to tell Monique everything—tell her the word they use for your son here. In Morocco.

But there is no word. There are only insults, Jaâfar.

There is the word *zamel*.

Don't say that word in front of me.

There is no other word. Only that, Malika. *Zamel*. You have to say it to Monique and explain it to her. Ahmed is zamel—gay. That's why he fled Morocco. He thinks that he can live freely in Paris.

There is no freedom, Jaâfar. Freedom doesn't exist. Neither here nor anywhere else.

Okay, Malika, let's stop our useless philosophizing. But you have to use the word. Zamel. It's the only word. Your son is in this word. I too am in this word. You want him to return and you won't even utter the word that describes him.

It's a dirty word.

There is only this dirty word.

It's dirty, Jaâfar, very dirty.

If you say it, Malika, this word won't be dirty anymore. At least among us four, you, me, Ahmed, Monique, through this letter . . . Say it . . . Say it . . . For me too, it will do me good to hear it come out of your mouth. Believe me . . . Go on, do this thing that your son Ahmed has awaited for so many years and that you never had the generosity to do.

I already told you that I won't apologize. I gave them everything. What more do they want?

You didn't give everything to Ahmed.

I am his mother.

Say the word. Say it. It's only a word. Zamel. Zamel.

Be quiet, Jaâfar. Be quiet. Let's get back to the letter.

I'm listening, Malika.

Dear Monique, here is Ahmed's old telephone number: 00 33 1 45 82 20 35. Maybe through this number you'll be able to find him. Paris can't be that big, I imagine. And besides, where there's a will, there's a way. So, please, find him and tell him that I only want one thing: for him to get back in touch with me. Tell him also that we only have one mother in this life. And that mother, me, is already old. And she will soon be gone for good. I don't have much more time to live. How much time? You already know my address in Salé. Here is my telephone number: 00 212 3 75 83 36 72. I'm counting on you, Monique. Find him. I've made mistakes with Ahmed, I admit it. But I didn't throw him in the street. I didn't stop him from going to school . . .

You're repeating yourself, Malika, without being specific.

I won't say the dirty word. Do you hear me?

Crystal clear, Malika.

Very good, Jaâfar.

Ahmed should never come back to Morocco.

Why do you say that?

You want him to come back and you can't even give him a word. Just a small five-letter word. Nothing. You want to give nothing. Sure, you have your reasons and, even over there, freedom doesn't exist, as you say. But Ahmed has to stay over there, far, far away. Far within France. Far within himself. And I'll stay here, far and just nearby: Zaki Prison. To each his prison.

Life is more complicated than that.

You speak only of yourself, Malika, and your own suffering.

But he's my son.

I have nothing more to say, Malika. We're at an impasse. Let's finish the letter with warm regards, okay? Maybe there's something else you want to add . . .

Yes.

What?

Monique, my son Ahmed is a bit peculiar. You'll understand.

Be gentle with him. When he was young, he often fell ill. His health is still very fragile, and I don't even know how he's tolerating the cold in France. Be gentle with him. And, if you can, make him speak. Make him tell you what I don't know about him. He might be more at ease with you. Tell him you were born in Morocco. Tell him your history with this country. Tell him what I could never tell him myself. The words he's been waiting for. A tenderness that I couldn't give him myself. Watch over him, from a distance, if possible. Invite him over during the Christian holidays to eat in your home. Do with him what I stopped you from doing with Khadija. Something might finally be mended, perhaps. Although solitude is everywhere, I hope my son Ahmed can find an open door with you sometimes, even briefly. A memory of his country. Another face from his country. I know that I'm asking you for a big favor. But you're the only person I know over there, on that land foreign to Ahmed. A land that is both unknown and intimate for me. The past between us cannot be forgotten, of course. But Ahmed does not seem interested in this past. He thinks only of himself, himself, himself. He has forgotten me. He's trying to do this impossible thing: forget his own mother. I write to you and I dare hope that this letter and these words will reach not only your hands but also your heart. Thank you in advance. Thank you and thank you again. Your father's grave in Rabat isn't far from us, I'll visit it from time to time. I'll clean it. I'll wash it. I'll bring Khadija with me. You can count on us. We will pray for your father, for his soul, with our language and our sensibility. *Salam* from Rabat, salam from Salé, to you and your family . . . Malika Kébir.

Is that all? Should I read the letter back to you?

No, Jaâfar. It's not worth it. Here's the envelope. Here's Monique's address. And here's the scarf, as promised.

Marwan will be very happy. Red is his favorite color. He'll be touched. I know, I hope. My heart isn't with me anymore. It still beats over there. It still roams over there. In the halls and between the walls of Zaki Prison. Marwan. I have no reason to stay here. Marwan is behind the walls. He still has another ten years. I'll find him again. I can only live over there. By Marwan's side. And so I have to finish this. I have the money, the scarf. I just have to plant this knife in your thigh. Theft, attempted murder, and a repeat offense. With a bit of luck, they'll sentence me to almost ten years. Like Marwan. Here you go . . . I wrote Monique's address on the envelope and your address too, on the other side. I'll mail this letter. You, Malika, you won't be able to.

The knife will be in my thigh, I know.

Don't lie to the police, Malika. Tell them everything. Accuse me of everything. Press charges. Don't hesitate. And give them my first and last name: Jaâfar Malki. Remember my family name, it's important. Malki. Malki. Tell them: Jaâfar Malki. Malki. And another thing . . . I've thought about it. I don't want you to be at the court for my hearing. Promise, Malika?

Promise, Ahmed.

I'm not Ahmed. I'm Jaâfar.

You are like Ahmed. You are so much like Ahmed.

And one more thing. I've changed my mind: don't ever visit me in prison, please.

Like him, you don't want to see me in the future.

I don't want to be attached to someone on the outside. No mother. I'm cutting ties. I keep cutting ties. For good. That's the only solution. Life, my life, is over there in prison. I don't want any hope.

You know my telephone number. Keep it on you. Or memorize it. You never know.

It's better to kill off hope now, right away. Hope complicates things in prison. I've already forgotten your telephone number, Malika. You won't come to see me. That's an order.

Who is Marwan?

He works in the prison kitchen.

A cook.

Yes. From Meknes.

Meknassi. They're crazy, the people from Meknes. How old?

Twenty-two.

Younger than you. He'll spend the majority of his youth in prison.

With me. By my side.

What a tragedy! All the youth of this country will disappear, will die in the kingdom's prisons.

This world is no longer my world, Malika. It's 1999. And it's only the beginning. I'm one of the pioneers, like I said. We're starting a new trend in Morocco. You'll see, doing prison time will soon be the coolest thing. The coolest and most tragic thing. We'll all lock ourselves up. And no one will be surprised. Ahmed would have been with us too, in Zaki Prison. But his cold, hard intelligence saved him. He left to conquer France. France will be mine! France will be mine!

"Saved," you say?

Marwan is tall, big, and dark. Very dark. He has enormous hands. Before him, the prison food was foul, inedible. Then he arrived, and everything changed. With the same ingredients, he performed miracles. Even the lentil dish that we were all sick of suddenly became so delicious. That's how I fell in love with Marwan. Through eating his food. Lentils with a bit of garlic, a bit of olive oil, and a few green peppers. I ate it all. Not just me: all the prisoners literally licked their plates that day. And we laughed. We sang and danced. We brought Marwan out. We carried him on our shoulders. We celebrated him. He was the king. Big and smiling. Sad and smiling. Broken and smiling. I fell for him at that very moment. Marwan, the king of Zaki Prison. He didn't pay any attention to me. And I hatched a plan for him to look at me, for him to see me and see in my eyes what I felt for him. I asked to work in the back kitchen. Washing the utensils three times per day. That way I was close to him and his light. I stole what I could of him. What wafted off of him nourished me. Dwelled in me. More and more intensely. Marwan. A body big all over. A large, large head. And magic hands. I dreamed at night of his hands, of my face in his hands, in the baraka of Marwan's hands. Everyone called Marwan Baraka in the beginning. When he came to the prison, he brought human warmth and the kitchen recipes he'd learned from his mother, El-Hajja Jamila. I'm not the one who cooks for you, no, it's El-Hajja Jamila: he always said that. After a month, everyone called him that, his mother's first name. El-Hajja Jamila. It didn't bother him at all. Moreover, it gave him protection in the entire prison. Marwan had brought love and sun into a sad, sordid prison. His hands and his meals scattered some sweetness everywhere, everywhere. And especially in my heart. But he still didn't see me. And I still didn't know how to get his attention. I . . . I . . .

That's it?

I'm sorry. Yes, that's it. I left prison two months after Marwan arrived. I miss him. So much. I've thought it all out. I'll go back to prison. And I'll ask to work in the kitchen as soon as possible. I'm sure they'll say yes. It's really hard work, in the kitchen. And not many prisoners want to do it. I'll volunteer. They'll have no choice. They'll accept. I'll enter Marwan's domain, El-Hajja Jamila's domain, Marwan's hours, Marwan's days and nights. I'll have a bed in the same cell block as him. I'll do everything to make it happen. My dream. My dream. Marwan's dark, round Meknassi body. I have no reason to stay here, Malika, on this side of life. I'll leave this merciless Morocco that does nothing for its children. I'll leave them their future plans and their economic prospects for the Morocco of tomorrow. Development and all the usual bells and whistles. I know none of that is for people like me. They've already killed me here, several times over. Now I want to live in the body and sweetness of Marwan. The miracle happened. Life is short. My chance is behind the walls. The walls of Zaki Prison and their wars, I'm used to it now. The prison and its hells, that's what I want. Darkness everywhere. Suspicion everywhere. Trafficking everywhere. Settling of scores. Beatings. Threats. Free prostitution. Bodies everywhere, everywhere, on top of each other. In the same odors, the same broken dreams. Honest prisoners at war against each other. And, despite everything, in solidarity. Tender, hard, merciless. Wild animals in tears. Thieves, murderers, old corrupt bourgeois men. Disgraced ex-ministers, tender Islamists, lost leftists, transgender singers, dancing drug lords. All together. All under the earth. Below ground. In accepted isolation. In the best-kept secret in the world. In another love that is free from the laws of the outside world. Another future, short and intense. And everyone, everyone adores Marwan. Our king. Our queen. El-Hajja Jamila.

Thank you, Jaâfar.

Jaâfar and Marwan. It's beautiful.

Yes, it's beautiful.

Thank you, Malika.

Thank *you*, Jaâfar. No one will ever tell me what you've just told me. Without shame. Without lowering their head or their eyes.

I'm sorry, Malika.

Don't worry. The knife in my thigh. I'm . . . Do it quickly. And leave quickly. Quickly . . .

I'll mail the letter to Monique. I won't forget. I promise. I have money to buy stamps.

No. No, Jaâfar. Don't do that. Don't mail the letter.

Are you serious?

Yes. Rip it. Rip it up. I don't know what came over me. I should never have dictated it to you. It's not a letter, it's submission, renunciation. I'll never bow down to anyone. Not to Monique or anyone else.

That letter is really smart, Malika. You hit two birds with one stone. You turn everything to your advantage. You help your son Ahmed in his conquest of France, and you shower Monique with such honeyed and sincere words that she'll have to help you. You come out on top, Malika.

Ahmed chose France. Let him figure France out on his own. Rip up the letter. I'm sixty-five now and I don't want to kiss the hands of those in power anymore. I gave everything. I built everything. I furrowed the paths of my children's lives for years. But, so far, none of them have proven themselves to be worthy of my sacrifices. Ahmed believes that freedom is the only thing worth pursuing in life. Who put that idea in his head? Not me. Not me. Freedom is only an illusion, an agenda, a false fiction. One day, he'll wake up. One day, he'll understand. On his own. Then he'll be so alone in the France that he chose, the France that won't ever really accept him. One day, he'll begin to cry without being able to stop and he won't have a gentle hand to caress his head, a sympathetic voice to pray for him in Arabic. No one. I'll be dead, dead. And then he'll have only memories tainted with sadness, filled with bitterness. He'll have only the distant past. Permanent regret. He's the one who cut himself off, he's the one who cut himself off. It's you, it's you, Ahmed, who cut yourself off. You changed your telephone number. You walked out of my life of your own accord. It's easy to look at others from on high and tell them that they've understood nothing, not about you, Ahmed, nor about your homosexuality, nor about the rest of the world. Ahmed, you chose. You chose. France took my first husband from me. And now, fifty years later, France is taking my son from me. Rip it up, rip it up, Jaâfar. That letter is a source of shame. Betrayal and submission. I'd rather die than do this thing which would destroy in one fell swoop all the struggles of my life. Rip it. Rip it. Ahmed has suffered, yes. Ahmed was raped, yes. Ahmed was beaten, yes. I saw it and I did nothing, yes. I regret it. And I apologize. I apologize. There you go. I said it. He is my son and he will always be my son. My son just the way he is. But I cannot abandon my convictions to indulge him and secure his supposed emancipation. I can't forget the past. My past that he himself does not even know. He was there at my side for years and he never had the generosity to ask me questions about me, my life before, what I lived through, my tragedies, my dark nights. And, one day, he wakes up, he comes to see me and says that he's going to France. He looks at me like I'm an insect that needs to be crushed, an ignorant, illiterate woman that needs to be removed from his path to success . . . I'm exaggerating perhaps, now. Perhaps. But I'm angry. Angry at him. I know that I'll die without seeing him again, without him giving me the chance to make amends for my mistakes. France is more important than me, that's what he's telling me. He made his choice, like I said. He cut himself off. Good for him. Shame on him. Rip up the letter, my dear Jaâfar. Rip it up. Rip it up. He'll come back when I'm dead and he'll have his share of the inheritance. He'll be entitled to a floor of this house that cost me my entire life to build. He'll come back then. Only then. He'll come back for the money. Four hundred thousand dirhams. He won't come back for me. No. Not that! He'll take the plane back only when I'm somewhere else. Done. A ghost. A grave. Ahmed is my son. He is so much like me in his harshness. But I can't bow down before him. I am who I am. Malika. I exist. I breathe. I eat. I think. I build. Ahmed, I see you. Ahmed, you don't see me. That's how life is: no one sees anyone. It's no big deal. It's no big deal at all. I fulfilled my role as mother. To a tee. I recognize this accomplishment. And even though my children don't see it as something valuable, I know what this role cost me. I was their mother. Even his, Ahmed. Even yours, Ahmed. One day, you'll see things clearly, very clearly. There you have it. Take out your sharp knife, Jaâfar. Plant it in my thigh.

After I leave, wait five minutes and then start to scream. Give my full name to the police.

I remember it. Don't worry. Jaâfar Malki.

Forgive me.

Go on. Do it, Jaâfar. Do it. Now is the time. The knife. The knife. Don't wait too long, don't think too much. Plant it in my thigh. Go on. And don't forget to take the scarf with you.

The scarf that will open Marwan's heart to me. Love with Marwan. Live in prison with Marwan. Breathe in prison beside Marwan.

My eyes are closed. Do it, hard. I'm not afraid of your knife. I won't die today.

Good luck, Malika.

Good luck, my son Jaâfar.